LEADLY
PROTECTOR

FEDERAL PARANORMAL UNIT

Book 4

NEW YORK TIMES and USA TODAY
BESTSELLING AUTHOR
MILLY TAIDEN

This book is a work of fiction. The names, characters, places, and incidents are fictitious or have been used fictitiously, and are not to be construed as real in any way. Any resemblance to persons, living or dead, actual events, locales, or organizations is entirely coincidental.

Published By

Latin Goddess Press

Winter Springs, FL 32708

http://millytaiden.com

Deadly Protector

Copyright © 2019 by Milly Taiden

Edited by: Tina Winograd

Cover: Willsin Rowe

Formatting by Glowing Moon Designs

All Rights Are Reserved. No part of this book may be used or reproduced in any manner whatsoever without written permission, except in the case of brief quotations embodied in critical articles and reviews.

Property of Milly Taiden

March 2019

Deadly Protector

Katrina Mejia knows she has to prove herself. As the newest member of the Federal Paranormal Unit, she's in a whole new world. She needs a lot of field time to get up to speed and is happy to take on any case. She'd also like more information on tall, dark and broody who makes her heart skip a beat and her panties shrivel into nothing.

Hunter Cross is content with the anonymity of working undercover. He's not a people person and isn't interested in a mate or a relationship of any kind. His heart is dead to emotions and he's more than happy to keep it that way. But things change when he finds his mate. A mate he doesn't want but craves.

Putting herself in the sights of a madman abducting women, Kat's about to become more than one man's prey. When a piece of Hunter's dark past shows up unexpectedly, it'll take more than his dragon to keep his mate alive. Danger takes center stage as Hunter and Kat team up to take down a predator while fighting their burning passion.

— For my danger-loving readers

Get yourself a dragon and tame him. He'll protect you for life.

ONE

Katrina Mejia knew he stood in the shadows, had known where he was the instant she entered the building. Strong. Commanding. Arrogant. The words literally flashed in her mind. Then his aura confirmed what she'd already guessed. He was aloof, a loner, and completely unapproachable. Why then was her body acting like it'd never been touched by a man? Okay, yeah, sure, it had been a while, but work was not the place. And it was damn sure not the day.

Her body went up in flames the closer to him she got. Being near him was like straddling the equator. Walking through the office, following Cynthia Vega to meet the infamous James Brock, she'd felt his eyes, the briefest strike of a match, before her body had gone up in flames.

It had taken a few days, but she'd found his name along with an extensive string of cases he'd solved while being undercover. So some of his standoffishness made sense. He was used to blending in, being part of the crowd, and watching instead of engaging. However, Kat wanted to engage with him...on a deep personal level.

Walking straight into Brock's office, she took a seat, pulled out the file full of papers she'd printed from her secured email in the middle of the night and waited. Seconds turned into long, tense minutes and all the while she could feel the man in the corner attempting to stare a hole in the back of her head.

An image of the man himself formed in her mind. Deep blue eyes, the color of an angry sea. Short dark hair with a sexy wave that just tipped the edge of the collar of his T-shirt. Speaking of T-shirt, God help that soft cotton as it stretched tightly across the defined muscles of his chest and biceps.

The little voice in the back of her mind said that Hunter Cross didn't work out. It was beneath him, or more likely, a complete waste of his time. Nope, his physique came naturally, and that was just sickening, but oh, so fine to look at.

Done with her useless fantasies, she blocked all thoughts of tall, dark, and dangerous instead

2

thinking about her first ever FPU briefing. Coming to the FPU before her thirtieth birthday was nothing short of miraculous. Director Vega pulled her right off the graduation podium and personally gave her the assignment. Never in a million years had she thought she'd get her first case so soon, but here it was and she planned on kicking its ass.

Every single tick of the large institutional clock on the wall added to her raging case of nerves. If the boss and the others took any longer...

"Damn, Mejia. Who you lookin' to impress?" Ramirez chuckled, looking extremely happy after his extended honeymoon. "You already got the job. No need to overdo it. Ya tryin' to make us all look bad."

She knew he was right. She was early and overly prepared. Had been getting ready for three days. God, she had no life. But none of that stopped her from getting up at three in the morning after going to bed at two and looking over the information for the meeting until she could recite every word verbatim. Being picked to be part of this special unit within the FBI had been a dream come true and there was no way she was fucking it up.

"Leave her alone," Jane Donovan, their team's tech guru and Ramirez's wife teased while swatting his hip when she walked by. "We were all the newbie once upon a time. Mejia just wants to start off on the right foot." The wink she included made Kat feel better, but the butterflies in the new agent's stomach were still dancing like they were listening to house music, and the thought of throwing up was soon to become a reality if the show didn't get on the damned road.

Recruited by Cynthia Vega, Kat was glad that only the director and her husband, James Brock, who also happened to be Mejia's new boss, knew about her abilities. Secrecy seemed to be the only constant in the team known as the Federal Paranormal Unit and that was just fine by her.

People never understood what she could do. Hell, she wasn't always sure. Most thought she was crazy and that had led to her keeping it a secret for most of her life. It was just easier that way. Explaining never seemed to work, and in most cases, made it worse.

Gripping the blue file folder like it was her only lifeline, she thought about the photos of the missing girls but it was the last one, Leslie Walton, whose face stayed in the forefront of her mind.

She was a carbon copy of all the others ~ light eyes, long blond hair, short and thin, and way smarter than the average bear. Hell, she had a Masters in Biomedical Engineering. Where could they all be? Was someone setting up a secret lab to create a whole new group of super soldiers to take over the world? Maybe they were concocting some crazy DNA and cloning the rest of the human race. Anything was possible, right?

What the hell? *I seriously have to stop watching late night cable. Mom was right, that shit is rotting my brain.* Besides, Kat had discarded all those theories somewhere between her second and third mug of coffee. Someone had targeted and taken those young women. Something bad was happening and she *refused* to rest until she brought them home, one way or another.

Remembering all the lists she'd written, the many pieces of yellow paper filled with details she'd written with her favorite blue pen and stuffed into her folder on her way out the door. Every damn one of them detailed all the things the girls did *not* have in common. Not one of them went to the same college. Not a one lived in the same town. They hadn't been Facebook friends, or followed each other on Instagram, or even followed each others' twitters. And it went on and on from there.

She'd only written two things in big bold letters in the middle of one sheet of paper. MISSING and LOOKS.

Snapping out of her own head and sitting up straight when the tall, dark-haired leader of FPU strode into the room, Kat refused to let her nerves show even as a cold drop of sweat made its way down her spine. Stopping only when he was standing behind his desk, the boss put his coffee down, and only when he had picked up Leslie's photo did he glance in her direction.

"I hope you all have taken the time to welcome Mejia to the team."

A rousing chorus of yes and sure filled the room as he looked at each person. All except for tall, dark, and asshole in the corner. Kat heard not a peep from that direction and had to admit that was fine by her. Of course, she was lying. There was almost nothing she wanted more than to hear his voice.

Turning the eight-by-ten glossy of Leslie that her parents' statements said was taken right before her graduation, Brock stated, "Anybody got any new information?" As silence was the only answer to his question, he stepped to the side, took what looked like the key fob for a car from his pocket, and pointed at the wall behind him.

Watching as the panels separated and a large video screen came to life, Kat's eyes moved from photo to photo. They there all were. All lined up in order of disappearance. Names in bold, black letter, dates of the last time they were seen in blue, when they were reported missing in red, and the name of the last person to see them in green.

"Donovan has gone through all their computers and their social media. She's even gotten their phone records since we don't have the phones themselves and the only thing even remotely linking one to another is their appearance and intelligence."

"And the fact that they all love biology and were really good at it, but chose not to be doctors," Donovan added.

Unwilling to keep her mouth shut even though that was probably what the newbie was supposed to do, Kat asked, "Isn't it weird that none of them even applied to the same colleges?"

Feeling all eyes on her, she went on, "I mean, okay, so they didn't live in the same towns or go to the same high schools, but we're talking about a hundred -twelve-mile radius and some really smart ladies who are all interested in the same subject. It seems impossible that their paths never crossed. Even if it was on a computer screen in some university registrar's office, they had to have been on the same list somewhere, didn't they?"

"Good call, Mejia," Donovan nodded. "But we checked. One or two, sometimes four or five, applied to the same places and another couple were contacted by the same recruiters or the same companies. But when we tried to connect all ten, excuse me ~ *eleven*, it was a dead end."

"Good thought, though," Brock encouraged, giving her a knowing look. "Got anything else?"

Not sure if she should say what she was thinking, a spike in energy from Strong and Silent in the corner had Kat's libido betraying her and her mouth opening before she'd time to overthink it. "What about the browser histories from their phones?"

Talking faster, not liking at all how the feelings of the man in the corner affected her, she hurried on. "I mean, I know you've checked their laptops and computers." She nodded at Jane. "But it seems to me that the only thing missing from any of these women's lives was a love interest. Could they have been using their phones to hook up? Or at the very least, talk to people they were interested in? Do the companies keep that information if it's not a text message? What if they had iPads or tablets? Is there a way to get that information?"

Out of her seat and racing toward the door, Donovan called over her shoulder, "Good call, Newbie." Then quickly added, "I'm on it, boss."

Looking up to find Brock smiling at her, Kat was finally able to relax. The weird vibes coming from behind her had settled and she could feel the approval of the others on her new team. It was a good feeling. One she hoped lasted.

"Good job, Mejia," Brock echoed her thoughts. "What else ya got?"

"Nothing right now, sir," she replied.

"Anybody else?" When the room stayed silent, he went on. "Then dismissed, but don't go far. As soon as Donovan has the information, I want each and every one of you pouring over those files. Find me something. The brass are breathing down my neck."

Reaching for the handle of her bag, Kat nearly jumped out of her skin when Brock added, "Don't go anywhere, Mejia."

TWO

"Hey, Cross, where ya been?"

"Here and there," he answered, not stopping to talk to Cash Callahan, a hawk shifter, all-around asshole, and the scummiest bottom feeder he'd ever laid eyes on. It sucked that the schmuck was the only person who'd been around long enough to remember Cross as anything more than a name on a roster, but then again, what the hell did it matter.

Being around so many people made his ass twitch and his dragon growl. There was a reason James Brock left him out in the field ~ it was safer for all involved.

Doesn't play well with others was at the top of every psych eval the FBI had ever forced him to take. Somewhere along the line the boss was able to get the bastards to lay off and the constant demands for interviews with the shrinks stopped, but that didn't change Hunter's attitude. Out of sight and out of mind was how he liked to play it. Undercover was made for him. And he was damned good at it too.

Nothing was going to stop him from returning to the field. Not even that curvy Latin lady with long, chocolate-brown curls and haunting hazel eyes. He didn't give a shit that she was his mate. The sooner he was on his Harley and driving the *opposite* direction, the better.

It didn't matter that he was walking slower than an eighty-year-old to keep his rock-hard cock from punching through his leathers. Or that his mirrored-lens sunglasses were covering the glowing elliptical pupils of his dragon. They'd have to cuff him to a chair if they wanted him to stay.

Love was for saps. Mates were for other people. Catching the scum of the earth was what he did, and a woman did *not* fit into his plan. No way, no how. Point blank. Period.

Pulling the vibrating cell phone from his pocket, he grumbled, "Cross."

"Get back up here. We've got a lead."

Before he could tell Brock to go to hell, there was a click and the line went dead. "Son of a bitch! I hate when he does that."

With his hand on the door and his eyes on his motorcycle, Cross knew he could leave and there wasn't a damn thing anyone could do about it. He was also well aware that James Brock who hunted him down with a single-minded doggedness would skin his hide just to prove he could.

Making a begrudging about-face, Hunter took his time heading back to the elevator. Huffing with irritation when the doors opened on the tenth floor, he watched her walk in and turn around. The fresh scent of woman mixed with honeysuckle had him simultaneously leaning forward and cursing under his breath.

Of all the fucking times to have not taken the stairs. Did this woman have radar or something? Would he look like a total dick if he stopped the doors from shutting and made a hasty exit? Of course, he would.

Letting his mind wander, Hunter couldn't help but imagine what it would be like to walk up behind Mejia, slide that form-fitting black skirt up her legs and bury his throbbing erection into her pussy. No sooner had the thought crossed his mind than the scent of her arousal filled the elevator.

Had he spoken aloud without realizing? Or was she as attracted to him as he was to her? Well, of course, she was. They were mates. It was the way their fucked-up world worked.

He thanked God when the doors opened, and his sexy woman headed straight out. He decided to compound his torture by following her back to Brock's office. The sway of her perfectly rounded hips conjured the most vividly erotic mental images of her naked, on her hands and knees, begging him to fuck her harder.

Deciding a trip to the bathroom to adjust himself was definitely needed, Hunter stopped dead in his tracks when Cash whispered, "Damn, I'd like to tame that wildcat."

Jealousy pushed both man and dragon to snarl aloud as his turn became a swerve and he was back on track. Feeling the scales of his beast flowing up his arms and across his shoulders, he pushed his sunglasses to the end of his nose and glared at Cash.

Swallowing so hard, his Adam's apple wiggled up and down, the slimy hawk shifter raised his hands in surrender, but still had the cheekiness to give Hunter a wink. "Watch it, asshole," he growled.

Getting to the large conference room less than a minute behind Mejia, he stalked to the back of the room. Waiting for the boss to arrive, his eyes stayed glued to the woman who would quite literally make him immortal, then scoffed, "Only the good die young. So, I'm bound to live forever anyway."

Ignoring the feel of Ramirez's eyes on him, it was a relief when Brock walked in with Donovan hot on his heels. Taking the lead, the spunky redhead handed a stack of folders to Mejia and asked that she pass them around.

Pissed that he was holding his breath, but knowing if he inhaled Kat's scent one more time, he would do something drastic, Cross held out his hand. "Thank you." Lower than usual and more of a growl than he liked, he hoped she hadn't noticed but was sure by the barely perceptible shiver that gave her hips a little extra shake, that she had.

"As you can see," Donovan started, "Mejia was absolutely right. Every single one of these girls was on the Two Becomes One dating app."

"Two Becomes One? Are you fucking kidding me? What a stupid name," Buchanan, a smartass at the best of times and worse now that he'd found his mate, scoffed.

"Shut up and listen or I'll send you to Asia with Villa," Brock ordered.

"Stupid or not, all eleven of our girls were on there." Donovan picked right up where the boss left off, not even looking up from her notes. "Now, they were all talking to different profile names from different IP addresses…"

"Then how is this a lead?" A tall, blond, pretty boy Agent Cross had never met, and didn't plan on talking to, asked.

"Let her talk, Sway," Ramirez growled, giving the new guy a glare before smiling at Jane and giving her a nod.

"Like I was about to say," Jane gave the blond a glare of her own, "they all had dates set up for the nights they disappeared and...hold onto your hats, people, every single one was meeting Prince Charming at the same bar." Stopping and looking around the room, she added, "And the computer picked up too many similarities in syntax, sentence structure, and word usage for it to *not* be the same guy."

Thumbing through the papers as the others talked amongst themselves, Cross damned near choked on his own tongue when his eyes landed on the name of the bar. "Beastly" was the hottest new bar in the area where humans could rub elbows with vamps, shifters, witches, warlocks, voodoo priests, and any other paranormal creature who wanted to play nice with the "regular folk." It was the stupidest thing he'd ever heard of and was just about to say so when a horrified gasp sounded from the front of the room.

Swamped in unbelievable sadness, wretched sorrow, and the feeling of loss that gripped his heart like a vice, Hunter's eyes shot to Mejia. In the span of a single heartbeat, she wheezed, "Angela's dead." Before her head fell to the side.

"What the..." Halfway across the room before he realized he'd moved, the dragon stopped dead when Brock bellowed, "Everybody out. Now!"

THREE

Opening her eyes and finding Brock and Vega staring at her like she was the opening act in the FPU's first freak show was bad. Then she could feel the creep in the mirrored glasses trying to burn yet another hole in her head and Kat thought about crawling under the table.

"Are you all right?" Vega's concern filled the room as the woman's mate, aka big, scary boss man, said at exactly the same time, "How long has this been happening?"

"Yep, I'm fine." Kat sighed, meeting Cynthia's eyes, not wanting to disappoint her mentor in any way. Then to Brock. She pushed herself up tall in the chair and nodded with a command she didn't feel. "Since I was little. Just wasn't ready for it this time. Sorry. Won't happen again."

Hand stretched across his forehead, the boss's tone softened as he rubbed his temples. "Nothing to be sorry about. I just have to know that you can handle the field assignments. I can't have you fainting in the middle of an op."

"No, sir. It won't happen again. I'll be prepared at all times."

As his hand fell away, Brock gave her a hard look, one she could feel all the way to the back of her skull, before slowly nodding. "Good. All you have to do is speak up, Mejia. Tell me or the Team Leader that you need a break. In the end, we're all in this together. Now, explain what happened and what you know."

Happy to put the focus back on the case and off her, Kat picked up her blue folder from where it had slid to the floor, laid it on her lap, and carefully removed the picture of the first girl reported missing. Laying it on the table, she took a deep breath, slowly let it out while counting to three then explained as her fingertips outlined the young woman's long blond curls.

"From the time I last looked at this photograph until when Donovan put her picture on the screen. So, about an hour and a half ago, Angela Thomas passed away."

"Just like that?" Brock stood and rolled his shoulders. "You get a feeling? A flash? A picture? How do you know?"

18

It was always the same question. She'd gotten really good at the answer.

"When I meet someone, touch something of theirs, or even see a picture of them, something in the depths of my brain *attaches* to the essence of that person. My *abuela* called it *clarividente* or clairvoyance. The priests said it was something more special than just a sixth sense. It was their belief that I have a sensitivity to the moment in time when a soul leaves its earthly body. In a nutshell, I've now met you. Let's say I never see you again, but fifty years from now, I pick up a newspaper and there's your picture."

"Okay, I'm with you."

"Just seeing your face would trigger my ability and I would know that you had passed."

"But if you never saw me again, you wouldn't know?" Brock sounded slightly intrigued but the look on his face said he'd heard way weirder.

"So, let me get this straight," Vega jumped in. "A hundred years from now, you pick up a box of pictures and just like that, you'll know who's dead and who's alive?"

"Yes, ma'am," she nodded. "That sums it up." Then needing to clarify, she added, "In most cases, I don't know right away. It just so happened that I was going through the file at home this morning and had looked at Miss Thomas's picture."

Pointing at the photo, he asked, "Any other info? Where is she? Was it a grisly death? Anything we can work with?"

Staring at Angela's smiling face, Kat looked into her light blues eyes and a feeling of peace flowed over her. No stress, just calm, serene peace. Angela had been happy, almost euphoric. It wasn't natural, but it didn't feel like drugs either. It seemed to come from somewhere in the young woman's brilliant mind. A suggestion...a command that someone had purposely placed there to keep her compliant and docile.

Relaying the information as quickly as her lips would move, Kat knew her words were running together but she needed to be sure they understood what she was picking up from the deceased. Never in her almost thirty years had she connected so closely with someone she'd never met.

"There's a fogginess to her thoughts. She's never had to second guess or fight to get a thought to surface, but she was most definitely doing that towards the end."

"Would you be able to get better information if you touched something that was hers? If you visited her apartment?" Vega was spitting out questions like bullets from a gun. "What if you talked to people she knew? Would her clothes give you a better connection? Any ideas?"

Jumping in when the director took a breath, Kat nodded, "Yes, most times any or all of those things can help but my perceptions will not be as clear as Agent Villa's. I won't experience what Angela did. I'm a spectator in their memories, and usually, one way up in the cheap seats. My ability is to feel if their soul still resides in the mortal coil. Make sense?"

"Absolutely," Brock barked as he marched across the room and opened the door. "Sway."

No sooner had the boss bellowed than the tall, blond, very easy on the eyes agent appeared in the doorway. "You called, sir?"

"I did. Get in here and shut the door."

Doing as he was told, Sway smiled in her direction as he crossed the room, stopping to the right and leaned against the wall as Brock stated, "I need you to go with Mejia to Nokesville."

"You got it, sir."

"Get your go-bag then checkout an SUV. You may need to stay the night."

"I'm on it." Moving with a grace that contradicted his six-foot-four-inch muscled frame, Sway looked over his shoulder and winked. "I'll be out front in thirty minutes. That good for you, Mejia?"

"Sure is. Thank you."

Waiting until he was gone, and the door was once again closed, Kat looked back at Brock as he began again, "I'll call ahead. You'll meet with their detective in charge. You should have his name in your file." Once again up on his feet and heading toward the door, he continued, "Play nice with the local LEOs, but make sure they know it's your show."

Grabbing the handles of her bag and springing out of her chair, Kat was halfway across the room by the time Brock had the door opened. Stopping in front of her boss, she nodded. "Thank you, sir."

"Good luck, Mejia," Vega appeared beside her. "Remember your training and trust your instinct. You'll be fine."

"Yes, ma'am. Thank you, ma'am."

Looking straight ahead, making a list of everything she needed to do and ignoring the fiery gaze of tall, dark, and silent, Kat made it to the elevator that was thankfully waiting and stepped inside. As soon as the doors closed, she slumped against the back wall, letting her head fall forward, and sighed. "Time to buckle up, *Muñeca*. This is the big leagues and you're up to bat."

FOUR

"What the fuck was I thinkin'?" Oz grumbled as they walked toward the horde of drunk and giggling women rubbing up on a couple of wolves, a panther, and a really young vamp on the patio of Beastly. "If I didn't owe you my life, I'd... "

"You would've still come." Hunter chuckled. "I heard your ears perk up the second I mentioned bar, free drinks, and drunk women with a thing for supes."

Barking out a laugh when his friend snickered, "Yeah, you're probably right," Cross couldn't help but think of all the dives from one end of the world to the other that he and Oz had raised their share of hell in and subsequently been kicked out of.

Army rangers for nearly ten years before

leaving the service and going their separate ways, Hunter had been sure to keep in touch with the explosives expert extraordinaire. Oscar Tomas Venegas ~ Oz to anyone who wanted to have their head remain on their shoulders ~ was crazy as a bedbug, could create a bomb out of anything from a piece of gum with a shoestring tied around it to a paper bag full of dog shit, and he was loyal to the very marrow of his bones.

Against all odds, because dragons from unaligned clans or different parts of the world almost always stayed clear of one another, Hunter and Oz had become brothers at first sight. No matter the situation, they had each other's back, even when one of them had been ordered to "play nice with the human groupies."

"I still can't believe they put a place like this out here in the middle of Nowheresville."

"Nokesville," Cross corrected just to irritate Oz. Who, as usual, ignored him and kept right on going.

"Cows on one side, pigs on the other, and plowed fields. The scent of fertilizer in the air. Were they playin' it safe? Thought one or all of us would flip out? Or were they tryin' to be different?" Chewing on his ever-present toothpick, Oz scoffed, "One thing's for sure, they didn't give a good gosh damn about security."

"It's all about the money. Out here is cheaper

than in the city," Cross grumbled.

"So, what's her name?"

"What?" Hunter tried to act shocked.

"Don't try to play a playa, asshole. I know when a woman's gotten the best of your scaly hide. So, spill. Ya know I'll find out sooner or later."

"No woman. Scout's honor." Hunter raised his hand and did the Boy Scout salute. "Hell, I haven't been laid in so long, I'm not sure I'd know which end to kiss and which to screw."

Shaking his head, Oz laughed out loud, "Yeah, right, and I've got some swamp land I'll sell ya real cheap." Keeping in step, the Latin Lover, as their squad had nicknamed him because he could talk a woman out of her pants before she knew what had happened, tapped the side of his nose. "The scent doesn't lie. You've at least brushed up against your lady love. That mating scent is riding you hard, brutha." Making a show out of pulling the toothpick from his lips and dipping his chin, he added, "Even the Lone Dragon can't escape destiny."

"Shut the fuck up, Oz," Cross grumbled. "Keep your eyes open and show off some scale. We need these ladies to fall all over us. It should draw our perp out if he's here. Profiler says he's a narcissist with a need to be the center of attention."

"Fancy words that all mean arrogant asshole who kidnaps and kills women to me," Venegas snickered. "But ya know how much I like showing off. So, off I go." Letting the midnight blue scales of his dragon flow down his arms and the pupils of his eyes elongate, he added with a waggle of his eyebrows. "Ladies love the Oz man."

Walking onto the patio as if he owned the place, the ladies' oohed and aahed, chittered and tittered, and basically made Hunter want to throw up on his own boots as they quite literally fell at Oz's feet. Following suit, the multi-colors of the paper lanterns haphazardly hanging around the tiki-esque perimeter reflected in the slick silver scales running down Cross's arms and covering the backs of his hands.

Immediately showered with attention, cold beers shoved at him from every direction immediately followed by shots of tequila and whiskey, it was the first time in his very long life Cross wished he could get drunk. At the very least, it would dull the high-pitched squeals and the feel of unfamiliar hands *all over* his body.

Pulled onto the dance floor and passed around for hours, he saw absolutely nothing and no one who piqued his senses. It was a total bust, just like he'd told Brock it would be. There wasn't enough time between kidnappings. The guy they were looking for was nothing if not meticulous.

From all the reports, the perp waited eight to ten days in every case. It had only been four since Leslie Walton was last seen. The sick bastard was still playing with his new toy.

"Last call. Last call for alcohol." The DJ's announcement sounded between one gyrating tune and the next.

"Thank God," he mouthed to Oz, who nodded, looking like he too was over all the attention. Waiting until his friend made his way to the bar, Cross asked, "You see anything?"

"Nah. You?"

"Nothing in..." The words froze on his tongue. She was there. No doubt about it. Both he and his dragon knew Mejia had just walked into the building.

"Cat got your tongue?" Oz joked.

"In a manner of speaking," Hunter growled, turning toward the door and zeroing in on the Ken doll who looked way too comfortable for the dragon's liking. "We've got company."

"Good company?"

"Don't know." Finding all five-foot-five of Kat making her way through the crowd of dancing women, Hunter paused. For the first time in his life, he had no clue what to do.

If he went to her, one of two things would happen. He would snarl and growl and they'd both be pissed. Or, well, the other possibility just couldn't happen so there was no reason thinking about it.

Deciding to cut and run, he gave a sharp nod to Oz and together they went out the way they came in. Walking in silence, Cross was sure he'd gotten away clean. Then Oz snorted. "Never thought I'd see the day when the fearless Hunter Cross tucked his tail and ran from a girl."

FIVE

"I still don't understand why we bothered driving all the way out here," Sway once again griped. "I told you they closed at midnight."

Looking out the passenger's side window as she tapped the nail of her index finger against her thigh, Kat muttered, "I just couldn't shake the feeling that something was happening out here."

"But you didn't see anything at Angela's, right?"

"No, I told you that." Turning, she glared at the side of his handsome face, too handsome if you asked her, and scolded, "How many times are you going to ask me the same questions?"

"Sorry." Sway glanced in her direction before looking back out the windshield. "This

29

whole profiling thing is new to me." Letting out a nervous chuckle, he went on, "Where I come from, we pretty much rely on the five basic senses with a little magic thrown in for good measure."

Wondering if she should tell him that she'd gotten a glimpse of his dragon scales on the back of his hands and the black fur of a panther on the nape of his neck while the ladies at the club were attacking, Kat decided to let him keep his mystique. Although, there would come a day when she would have to satisfy her curiosity and ask how exactly his parents met.

Moving on to the important part of what Sway had said, she nodded. "I hear ya. Profiling isn't what I thought I'd be doing when I joined the FBI, but I have to admit, I feel like it's the right place for me. Especially with this case."

When his only response was silence, Kat slid her eyes to the side and snuck a peek. Shocked to find him scowling and biting his lips, she blurted out, "What's wrong? What's got your tail in a tangle?"

"Ha! Good one," Sway laughed. "I like that. I may just have to steal it."

"It's what my *abuela* used to say when she'd find me thinkin' too hard." Tilting her head to the side and giving him her *don't bullshit a bullshiter* look, she added, "Like you were just then."

"Busted," Sway snickered. "Yeah, all right, I was just thinking, do you really think we'll be able to pick this guy out of a crowd? Isn't one of the reasons these disappearances went unnoticed for so long the fact that he *doesn't* stand out? He's just a regular Joe, or he makes himself appear like a regular guy?"

And for the first time, Kat actually thought of Sway as more than just a pretty face. It was refreshing and gave her an outlet for everything swirling through her brain.

"You're right. And I don't believe I was being led to Beastly to find *him*." She blew out a sharp breath. "It was more to see the place itself. To understand how a beautiful, intelligent young woman, eleven attractive, smart women, with bright futures, their whole damn lives, could be lured to Backass, Nowhere, just to mix it up with shifters and vamps."

Pulling the stack of photos from her bag, she tapped them against the palm of her free hand. "Do you think these ladies fit the demographic of the ones tryin' to get you outta your Levis?"

"Nope, not at all."

"Exactly. And why a dating site? Everyone we talked to said Angela had plenty of eligible men in her life. Donovan found evidence they all did. What possessed them to go online, give up personal information about themselves, and then drive to Nokesville, of all places, to meet up with a guy they'd never met? It doesn't fit what we know about the victims."

"Nope."

"What if—" The sound of her phone ringing had her digging in her bag to retrieve the device. Swiping the screen, she answered, "Ma'am?"

"What have you found so far?" Vega's tone was direct. "Anything we can use?"

"Just confirmation of what we already know. Angela was top in her class. Doing great at work. Her apartment was neat and tidy which fits the profile we've built. Her bills were paid. Her landlady said she had several gentleman suitors and always seemed happy."

"Anything else I should know?"

It was obvious Vega already knew the answer, but Kat had to wonder how. Was she having them followed? Were they chipped? Did the boss lady have the eye?

Deciding it was better to just give it up then take the chance of having her ass kicked, Mejia confessed, "I twisted Sway's arm and had him take me out to Beastly."

"And?"

Just as she'd suspected, there wasn't the slightest surprise or hesitation in Vega's voice.

She'd known exactly where they were. But how? Hurrying on, Kat explained, "It just doesn't fit. There was absolutely nothing in Angela's belongings or apartment to suggest she had any interest at all in shifters, or any kind of supernatural. Why then would she agree to go out to that bar, off the beaten track, to meet someone she didn't know other than from the internet?"

"Good questions. Got any answers?"

"No, ma'am, but I'll work on it."

"Good," Vega asserted. "Briefing in conference room A at nine a.m."

"Yes, ma'am."

Taking the phone from her ear and thinking about what the director had just said, or more to the point what she hadn't said, Kat turned in her seatbelt and blurted, "What if they had talked? What of all their communication hadn't been through messaging?"

"What are you saying?" Sway asked as he maneuvered the SUV onto Aden Road. "Donovan checked all their phone records. No numbers matched."

"I know that. But at least it would explain why these usually cautious women walked blindly into a trap."

"That it would." Once again narrowing his

eyes, something Kat now knew meant he was thinking, Sway added, "So, what's your plan?"

"I'm gonna ask Brock and Vega to let us go undercover."

SIX

"You got a minute, boss?"

He breathed a sigh of relief when Brock nodded. "Yeah, come on in. To what do I owe this honor?"

Ignoring the dig, knowing it was meant to remind him that he rarely, if ever, made contact unless forced, Cross got right to the point. "Last night was a total waste of time."

"And you're here to say, 'you told me so'?"

"No fun when you already know I was right." He gave the boss a half grin, his idea of being nice.

"You always were a sick son of a bitch who had to do everything the hard way." James snorted. "Now, get on with it. We've got a briefing in ten and I have phone calls to make in the meantime."

"We're not gonna draw this guy out by dancing around a club. He's methodical, prepared, and definitely not into guys. You're barking up the wrong tree if you think he wants attention and us being there will make him uncomfortable, on the contrary.

"If he was there last night, he ate it up. We drew all the attention and made it easy for him. But I don't think he was anywhere near Beastly. It's too soon. He has a system. One he thinks he's perfected, and he's not gonna deviate from that plan. You need an undercover. Someone who can play his game, just not get caught."

Stopping as Brock raised his hand. "You're right, and we've got it covered. That's what we'll be going over at the briefing." Standing, he went on, "I'm gonna want you in on this. You've been out there. Have the lay of the land. Won't alert any of the regulars or the bar staff."

Leveling his gaze, the boss warned, "But only you. I've got no problem that you took a buddy of yours out there last night, but from this point forward, it's FPU only. I can't take a chance that someone will fuck up and tip this bastard off."

Pissed that James's nose was way too far up in his business, Cross gave a mock salute and sarcastically agreed. "Sir, yes, sir."

Not looking up, Brock dismissively grunted, "Thanks. See you in conference room A at nine...sharp."

For the hundredth time, Hunter wondered why the hell he put up with the bureaucratic bullshit of the FBI, of FPU, of James Brock, of civilization as a whole. All he had to do was give the whole fucking mess the middle finger, don his scales and wings, and head back to Scotland.

"Haven't been there in fifty years or so, but the place *is* still mine," he grumbled to himself, picturing the heather covered fields surrounding his family's castle.

"Excuse me?"

Wrapping around him like dark satin sheets, her soft dulcet tones forced every drop of blood flowing around his brain to rush southward with wild abandon. Stepping forward before he knew he was moving, Cross stopped mid-stride when Kat's next question woke him from his lust-inspired fog. "What did you say? Were you talking to me? Sorry, I wasn't paying attention."

Shadows underlined her expressive hazel eyes that crinkled at the corners as she shyly smiled. Paying closer attention than he wanted, the pallor of usually glowing skin and the cup of black coffee she was balancing atop a stack of papers made his protective instincts kick into overdrive.

She was exhausted. Not that it took anything from her beauty or the magnetic attraction that drew him in like a moth to a flame, *nope,* not even a little bit. It did, however, skate across his every nerve, making him wonder what the hell she was doing when she should have been sleeping.

Visions of Sway holding her in his too-perfect arms and kissing her puffy pink lips as the dickhead worked his way into her bed had Cross's jaw clenching so tightly, he was waiting for a tooth to break. Needing to know for sure, he went ahead and closed the distance between them, forced a smile, and as bad as it hurt, made small talk. "No, sorry, I was talking to myself. Sometimes I need the expert advice."

"Oh," she chuckled, that sound like the tinkling of little silver bells made his heart skip a beat. "No worries. I do that a lot."

Taking a good, long whiff and scenting only the soft, fresh notes he knew from memory were part of Kat's chemistry, Hunter took a step back and held out his hand. "Name's Hunter Cross. Sorry, I meant to do that ear…" Unable to finish his sentence as sparks flew up his arm, spun around his chest, and landed right in his crotch from the simple touch of her fingers to his, he stood unmoving and silent.

Oblivious to his discomfort, Kat shook his hand and smiled. "No worries. I should've introduced myself yesterday. Katrina Mejia, but you can call me Kat."

Immediately aware of the loss as she took her hand from his, Hunter regretted having ever touched her. But knew he would do it again if given half a chance. She was his kryptonite. Someone he had to avoid at all costs, because if he did ever have the chance to touch her again, there would be no letting go.

Pulling on his years of training and steely control, all he could do was nod. "Nice to meet you." Motioning toward the conference room, needing to put some distance between himself and the alluring distraction he wanted no part of, Cross added, "See ya in there."

Dead on her feet, she smiled. "Yeah." Then turning, she added over her shoulder, "Nice to meet you, too, Hunter."

His name on her lips was pure torture. His dragon pushed hard against the confines of his skin as if to say, "You may not want her, but I damn sure do."

Forcing the beast back, Hunter was hypnotized by the seductive sway of her hips and the way her jeans caressed her curves. Imagining all the ways he could strip her right out of her clothes and satiate his throbbing erection, Hunter refused to give into the mountain of feelings falling around him. Bracing himself and rolling his shoulders to release the tension, he stared straight ahead and walked in her wake.

Entering the room, he took his usual spot in the back of the room seconds before Brock and Donovan entered. Not one to mince words, the boss got the briefing swiftly underway. "I'm turning this over to Donovan and Mejia. They've been working all night on some new information. Their plan of attack will flush this guy out."

"All right, both Mejia and Cross were out at Beastly last night," Donovan said, activating the large viewing screen to her right.

Kat's eyes flew to his. He could see the questions, almost like accusations but refused to acknowledge them. No explanations were needed. They were two agents doing their jobs, following orders, trying to catch a sicko. That was all she needed to know.

"From Cross's report," Donovan went on, "we know there are exits here and here and here." She clicked buttons on the gadget in her hand and red dots appeared at every door. "There are private booths with curtains here, and secluded VIP rooms here. The rest is all out in the open ~ dance floor, bar, and patio. Those areas won't be hard to watch. They have pretty good security, but nothing I can't hack."

Turning back to the room, she smiled. "So, that's it for me. Mejia's gonna run through the logistics and timeline."

Eyes glued to his mate, unable to fathom why a new agent with little to no experience would be running an op of such importance, Cross listened closely for clues. There was no doubt Kat was more than she appeared, hell, everybody in FPU was, but there was something else there...something just out of his reach.

"It's been five days since Leslie Walton was reported missing. We can assume that she was abducted less than twenty-four hours prior based on the other victims and the fact that she was at work, didn't miss any appointments, and picked up her standing order of Thai. With that in mind, Donovan and I set up a user profile on Two Becomes One early this morning and we've already had several hits."

Impressed that her mind worked along the same lines as his, Hunter thought, *Look at that. Girl's got a brain and knows how to use it.*

"At this point," Kat continued, "we're trying to see who's interested in talking." Opening her hands, they moved as she spoke. "The dating site's server doesn't keep logs of their users' interactions, but we know he is doing way more than just chatting on the computer. I believe he is actually convincing them to *make contact* via phone call."

Leaning her hip against the corner of the

table, she continued to talk with her hands which Hunter found adorable no matter how hard he tried to deny it. "He spoke with our girls. That's the only thing that makes sense. He lulled them in with a false sense of security, made them feel safe to trust him."

"If not on the phone directly, through some voice app or using different burner phones." Letting her fingertips fall to the top of the table, her nails tapped a deliberate rhythm. "These young women wouldn't have just gone off half-cocked to basically the middle of nowhere to meet a virtual stranger. These have to be the pieces we are missing."

Taking a deep breath and squaring her shoulders, Kat turned back to the screen, pointing to six photos of men who looked pretty normal, or as normal as a guy who's picking up women on the internet can look. "These men almost immediately made contact with Felicity Jones, our alias profile. All in less than ten minutes of us going live. That tells me that they are regulars. They more than likely work a nine to five job and spend their nights searching for love...or a reasonable facsimile."

Nodding to Donovan who made four of the pictures fade to black, Mejia continued. "These two were extremely casual. To the point that it felt well-rehearsed, almost rote. There were no stops and starts as they typed their questions and answers. It was like they had a script and were following it to the letter."

"Isn't that normal for guys trolling a website for dates? They've done it so often, they just follow the same routine and talk to whoever talks back?" Sway asked, giving Kat a wink that had Hunter clenching his fists and wondering if anyone would truly miss the Ken doll if he tore the jerk into tiny pieces and dumped him in the landfill.

"In some cases, but with these two, it was methodical, and from the transcripts I'm going to pass around..." She paused, picked the same stack of papers Hunter had seen her carrying earlier and handed them to Ramirez. "You'll see that the questions are exactly the same. Yes, a few of the words have been changed but they mean the same thing."

Pointing back to the screen as Donovan put the transcripts side-by-side, Kat explained, "See, it's the same sequence. The person is leading Felicity. He takes her right to the edge then says he has to go, but not before he sets a time for them to talk again."

"And he signs off with *I'll be waiting*," Cross mused aloud.

"Exactly!" Kat's excitement was palpable. Pointing directly at him, she was obviously thrilled that someone was actually following along and understanding where she was going. "If he keeps to the timetable, there are only three days left for him to convince her to speak to him and agree to meet at Beastly." Glancing at Brock before looking at everyone in attendance, she beamed. "And that's when I'm gonna reel him in."

SEVEN

He'd spent two and half days barking at everyone who dared to look his way, spending the nights pacing the floors, and jumping at every noise near and far. Knowing that on this night he'd have to watch Kat meet the man they were at least partially sure was abducting women had Cross so wound up, he was having trouble controlling his dragon. Something that hadn't happened in centuries.

Pacing the pool deck behind his house, he watched as scales flashed up and down his arms before immediately disappearing in sync with the ragged beat of his heart. "This is why the whole fated mate thing is for the fucking birds." Dropping into the redwood lounger, he grunted, "I'm not doing it. I can't deal with a mate. I'm driving myself fuckin' crazy and I haven't even spoken ten words to her."

Cursing when his phone alerted him to an email, Hunter read the subject of the email aloud, "Op Briefing in 1 Hour." On his feet and heading toward the sliding glass door, he grumbled, "Happy, happy, fuckin' joy, joy."

Reminding his dragon the entire twenty minute drive to the office that they were *not* having anything to do with Katrina Mejia, he'd just pulled into the parking lot when that very woman stepped out of her car. Shutting the driver's side door then opening the back, she bent over at the waist and leaned in.

Captivated by the sight of her perfect ass, Hunter was forced to swerve to miss an oncoming car then veer sharply in the opposite direction to avoid ramming into a parked one before using his considerable strength to stay up on two wheels. Parking his Harley, he made putting down the kickstand, getting off the seat, and opening his saddlebags take as long as possible.

Once he was sure Kat had made her way into the building, he shot toward the back entry. Swiping his badge, he took the stairs two at a time and ducked into the conference room before anyone else arrived.

"What an effin' loser," he scoffed under his breath. "Actin' like a teenager in heat. This shit ends right here and right now. I'm a slave to no one, not even my own instincts."

"Talking to yourself, old man," Sway joked, entering the room and making a beeline in Hunter's direction.

Pulling the only chair near him closer, Cross plopped his feet on the seat, crossed his ankles, and with a shit-eating grin nodded. "Hell yeah. I'm the only one worth talkin' to around here."

Not easily deterred, which made Cross hate him just a little more, Sway's hand landed on the back of the first chair he walked past. Shoving it ahead, he placed it way too close for Hunter's comfort and plopped down before agreeing. "I hear ya." Swiping his palms down his thighs as his eyes slid side-to-side, he went on. "You ready for tonight? I hear it's just you, me, and Kat in the club. Think it's gonna work?"

There was something in the shady way Sway kept scanning the entrance and the weird cloud of flop-sweat and worry that had Cross asking, "Why wouldn't it?"

"No reason." Eyes still roaming the room but landing on nothing, the younger agent vacillated. "It's just that, well... Mejia has no experience. That place is always wall-to-wall people. The music is loud and thumping. The whole thing is rushed and based on information that's spotty at best."

The longer Sway spoke, the harder Cross listened. Not to the Ken doll's words, but the racing of his heart, the hitch in breath, and the anxious tap of the heel of his shoe against the hollow leg of his chair.

Slowly turning his head, Hunter watched a single bead of sweat wind its way out from under Sway's messy blond hair and down his cheek before disappearing under his chiseled jawline. Pushing his enhanced perception straight into the younger shifter's mind, he saw the spark of a dragon alongside the sinewy grace of a black panther and watched as both struggled to be set free.

Pretty boy was nervous, and it wasn't because he was a mix of two very different animals. No, he'd overcome that years ago. He was scared...*scared shitless* and looking for a way out. Sad thing was, his animals were ready to take over and deal with whatever threat was bearing down on them. If Ken doll wasn't careful, those predators with whom he shared his soul would win, and the losers would be dead.

Trying to think of a way he could ask what was going on without admitting what he'd just done. Or better yet, alert the boss that Sway was freaking the hell out, again without calling attention to himself, Hunter knew he'd drop that dime in a hot second. The pretty boy was only there to back up Kat. If he wasn't on his game, she could get hurt or worse, and then Cross would be forced to kill him. It was as simple as that.

Of course, if Hunter did tell Brock then he'd have to admit that he'd broken the cardinal rule of FPU. He'd breached someone else's mind without their knowledge or consent. It was considered treason and carried a death sentence.

"Might be easier," he sighed.

Thankfully, Brock, Donovan, and Kat led the parade of participants into the room, effectively giving Hunter time to come up with a plan. Trying to shake the notion that he could just slip back into Sway's mind and find out what had the three-natured Ken doll all messed up, he tuned in as the boss ordered, "All right, people. Let's get this show on the road." Looking at his watch, he added, "We've got two hours before you people need to head out. Quiet down and listen up. We've got no time for any bullshit."

Stepping forward, her excitement unmistakable as she began catching everyone up. "I hope y'all have been following the emails we've sent over the last couple of days." Her gaze captured Hunter's making him squirm in his seat. "Only one of our suspects went forward with verbal contact and after the second call asked for a date."

The heat in her eyes, the conviction in her tone, the way her body vibrated with excitement was so alluring, so intoxicating, Hunter had to shift in his seat to keep the impression of his zipper from being permanently tattooed into his erection. Finally, he was able to breathe when she looked away, he glanced to the side to find Sway gone.

Searching the room, he caught Ramirez's eye and mouthed, "Where's pretty boy."

Throwing his thumb over his shoulder, the white tiger mouthed, "Taking a leak."

Nothing about what was going down made sense and it damn sure didn't set well. Shit was spinning out of control. Hunter may not want a mate, but he damned sure wasn't letting anything happen to her. Dragons had a commitment to protect humans. That was his story and he was sticking to it.

On his feet the second Brock dismissed the group, Cross followed the scent of the shitting-in-his-shorts shifter. Nowhere to be found on their floor, or the two above and the two below, Hunter decided it was time to alert the boss when Sway appeared out of nowhere. Suddenly calm, cool, and collected, the Ken doll smirked, "What's up, old man? Lost again?"

Lunging forward, Cross caught himself a split-second before he slammed Sway against the wall. Nodding to the boss, noting the pointed look and furrowed brow, he added, "I'll be ready."

Waiting until the door to Brock's office was closed, Hunter shot a fiery look at the cocky pretty boy and growled through gritted teeth, "Watch your back, asshole."

EIGHT

Unable to shake the feeling that something was happening between Sway and Cross, Kat decided it was better to find out what was going on before they were out in the field. Looking everywhere for one or both of the testosterone-laden men, she stood outside a locked door where hushed voices were having a heated debate.

Reaching for the doorknob, she jumped back when someone shouted, "Kat! Agent Kat Mejia? Are you down here?"

Plastering on a smile and heading back the way she'd just come, Kat popped out into the huge common area at the same time a redhead dressed completely in black leather smiled and waved. Bouncing over, her green eyes sparkling with glee, she held out her hand and chattered,

"It is so nice to meet you. Director Vega has nothing but great things to say about you. My name's London, London Connor and I'm…"

"You're the analyst who linked the missing persons cases." Shaking the woman's hand, Kat said, "That was some fantastic work. You have an amazing eye for detail. I hope you're getting a commendation."

With her smile stretching wider and a blush covering her cheeks, London shook her head. "No big deal. Just doing my job." Letting go of Kat's hand, she stepped closer and whispered, "What I really want is to come up here. Computers and data are cool, but my dream is to be a field agent."

"I don't think that'll be a problem. You're a smart cookie with a good head on your shoulders."

"Thanks so much. I can't tell you how much I appreciate you saying that." London beamed as she handed Kat a large yellow envelope. "I found some other information that might be helpful."

"Great!" Taking the envelope, Kat went on, "Thank you so much. I'll let you know as soon as I've had a chance to go through it."

"Cool." London opened her mouth to say something else, but the chirp of her phone had her saying, "London here." Before placing her hand over the mouthpiece and whispering to Kat, "It was great to meet you. Talk soon."

Waving as the young woman sped away, Kat looked down at her watch and sighed. "No time to find out what's going on with Tweedle-Dee and Tweedle-Dum."

Pushing all thoughts of Hunter Cross from her mind, she headed to the tech room to be fitted for her mic and earbud. With every step, the feeling grew that she was still missing something. Checking the photos of the girls at least once an hour every hour for the last three days, she was absolutely certain no one else had passed away. Why then, hadn't Angela's body been found?

What she knew of their perp, hopefully the suspect she was meeting tonight, fit the profile of a narcissist. If he had any empathy at all, he wouldn't be abducting women in the first place. There was no remorse because there were eleven missing ladies. Guilt and shame would've forced him to stop, or at the very least let the women go. That hadn't happened, and she had to believe he was still hunting...collecting...creating his own harem?

Taking a deep breath, she inhaled the warm smoky scent belonging to Hunter Cross. No matter what she did, how many times she told herself he was an arrogant asshole who didn't deserve a second of her attention, she couldn't stop thinking about him.

There was just something about him. It was like the tough, macho I-don't-need-anybody façade was all an act. That he had a heart and soul and was capable of so much more than he wanted anyone to know. God knew he was sexy as homemade sin and twice as lethal to her sanity.

One look, hell, even a glance and Kat couldn't catch her breath, her body shook with need, and her pussy was wet and aching. Why was she always attracted to the assholes? What was it about bad boys with bad attitudes who couldn't admit they were human that had her ditching every iota of common sense and panting like a cat in heat?

"I'm an idiot. That's what," she groaned under her breath, grabbing the handle of the tech room door and disappearing inside before she was forced to talk to the sexiest man on two legs.

"You look like you need a drink," Donovan teased. "Nervous about tonight?"

"I wish it were that easy."

Suddenly concerned, Jane got to her feet and closed the distance between them. "Somebody giving you a hard time? Just say the word and I'll have Ramirez kick some ass."

"No, no, no," Kat shook her head. "It's nothing like that. But thanks. I appreciate you having my back. What's bothering me is that I can't figure out why we haven't found Angela's body, or come close to where he might be keeping all these women."

Blowing out the breath she hadn't realized she was holding, she went on, "What's he doing with them? I would say he's a collector, but that doesn't ring true." Pushing off the door and pacing the room, she thought out loud. "He's doing this for a reason. He's got a plan. He does *nothing* without a plan."

Tapping her temples with the heels of her hands, she had to keep going, had to keep reasoning through what was bothering her, or it would cloud her focus for what she had to do later that night. "Why do kidnappers abduct? What is their motivation?"

"Ransom. Replace someone they lost," Donovan responded. "Complete a fantasy. Force a relationship. Torture and kill. Take power when they feel powerless. Control another to take control of their situation."

"Yes, but do any of those feel right? And if they do, why eleven women? That's a lot of people to take care of, to be responsible for. And why still be hunting? Why kill... wait! Did he kill Angela?"

"Dunno. You said she was dead," Jane answered.

"I know, but I don't know how or why. Only that she wasn't afraid and felt euphoric." Getting more excited with every second, sure she was about to latch onto another piece of the puzzle, Kat raced across the room. Grabbing a pen and paper as she sat and started to scribble as fast as she could.

Writing the initials of each of the girls, she started to reiterate what they already knew, making her own abbreviations beside each set of letters. Everything matched leading to the same dead end.

Then a spark, a flash of a memory she hadn't realized she had, popped into focus. She'd seen something in Angela's apartment, something that until that moment hadn't materialized because it hadn't been relevant.

Spinning in her chair, she held up the paper and as she was underlining the last word she'd written with the tip of her finger she said it aloud, "Inhaler." Out of the chair and dashing to the door, she continued. "There was the cap to an inhaler in the top drawer of Angela's bedside table. No one would've known what it was. I didn't know what it was until right this second."

Spinning on her toes, needing to finish her thought and calm down before she approached Brock, she went on. "I'm sure everyone who went through that room thought it was trash. I know I dismissed it, but now I can see it as clear as a bell. I know what it was because my roommate at boarding school used to leave those effin' caps all over the place. I would step on them in my bare feet on my way to the bathroom in the middle of the night and want to smother her in her sleep because it hurt so damn bad."

Making the shooing motion with both of her hands, Donovan commanded, "Go! Go, girl, go! Tell the boss. This is important shit."

"Thanks, Jane," Kat hollered over her shoulder. "Thanks for everything."

NINE

"Hunter, get in here." The boss's shout had Cross cursing as he turned the corner and crossed the threshold into his office.

"You bellowed, sir?"

"Get in here and shut the door."

Eyes glued to Brock, refusing to look at either Sway or Kat, Cross kicked the door shut with the heel of his boot and stood where he stopped. "Done and done."

"Tell him what you remembered, Mejia."

The sound of Brock's stern order made the hairs on the back of Hunter's neck stand on end. This fucking op couldn't get over fast enough. There were too many moving parts, not enough information, and a woman who caused him to lose focus.

Distance was the only thing that would cure what ailed him. Hundreds and hundreds of miles between himself and that sexy little Latina before he was FUBAR and fell in love with her. God knew he already wanted to protect her from everyone, including herself. Sappy, stinking love would throw kerosene on an already blazing fire.

"Yes, sir." The sultry sound of her voice made his cock jump in his jeans. Just another reason he needed to get the hell outta Dodge, like yesterday.

"I was talking to Jan...I mean, Donovan. It's been driving me crazy that we haven't found Angela's body. I mean, nine times out of ten, kidnappers will get rid of the evidence of a botched abduction as soon as possible and work as hard and as fast as they can to replace what they've lost. At least, that's the profile for single victim abductors."

Watching as she took a drink from the water bottle she was holding tightly, the glistening of her lips made Cross's dragon roar. Dammit all to hell and back, Mejia was going to the death of him.

"Ours is highly organized. . ." She was already talking again by the time Hunter forced enough blood back to his brain to comprehend her words. "And we now know, not in a hurry. If he had been, another woman would've been taken the same day or the next after Angela's passing."

Tapping her bottom lip, she reiterated, "He thinks he's smarter than we are. He's continued to follow his schedule even though one of his victims died. But…" she paused, and no matter what he did, Cross couldn't help but lean forward until she began again. "That's because *he* didn't kill her."

"What? How the hell could you know that?" Sway said, his voice rough and gravelly as he sported a scowl.

Looking shocked, and if Cross wasn't mistaken, disappointed by Sway's crass attitude, Kat instantly slapped on a mask of indifference, but she couldn't quell the flames flashing in her hazel eyes as she deadpanned, "Because we missed something when we were in her apartment."

"No way, we…"

"Shut up and listen," Brock growled. "You missed something. Regardless of what you think, you're far from perfect. Mejia figured it out. Deal with it."

"*We* missed it," Kat stressed. "And it was the cap of an inhaler. I saw it but it didn't register." Once again using her hands to talk, she clarified, "Don't you see? If there was a cap, then there had to have been an inhaler sometime or another." When no one immediate answered, she said, "Angela was an asthmatic. She either didn't have her inhaler or used it all after being taken. There no way he could've known and no way he could've taken care of the problem."

"So, you're saying he had no intention of ever killing her?"

"Yes," she nodded and smiled, making Hunter's heart stutter in his chest. "Yes, Hunt...Cross," she quickly corrected herself. "His intent is to keep them, not kill them."

Caught up in her enthusiasm and in awe of how her mind worked, his mouth was open before his brain engaged and he asked, "But why? Does he think he's a sheik and needs a harem?"

Laughing out loud, the sound so sweet Hunter smiled right along, enjoying the way her cheeks blushed and her eyes danced. "That's what I thought." At the sound of Brock clearing his throat, Kat immediately schooled her features. "To be honest, I haven't figured that part out yet."

"And she doesn't have time right now," the boss interjected. "You all need to get wired and outta here. All your questions will be answered when you catch this asshole." Stopping and staring again almost immediately, he barked, "I'll have Donovan check Angela Thomas's medical records."

"Yes, sir. I think she might already be working on that," Kat nodded, giving Sway a wide berth before zipping past Hunter.

Not ready to let the younger shifter off the hook for any of the bullshit he'd pulled, Cross stepped in front of Sway and using his first name, something he rarely did with people he didn't know or didn't like, spat, "Get your head outta your ass, Wyatt. If you can't handle this mission, I'll tell the boss to make you stand down."

Rolling his eyes and stepping to the side, Sway purposely bumped Cross with his shoulder and scoffed, "Try it, old man, and see what happens."

Prepared to rip the Ken doll into tiny pieces, Hunter stopped short when Brock rumbled, "Cross, I need a word."

TEN

Parking outside Beastly, Kat took a second to make sure she was prepared to act like any other woman on her way to meet a man she'd only ever spoken to on the phone. The little voice in the back of her mind continued to chat, *"He's not gonna look like that picture on the dating site."*

But Jane had checked it every way she knew how and confirmed the photo had not been doctored. Of course, that didn't mean he hadn't swiped it from someone else. It was only logical explanation she could come up with for "Craig Neilson" to say, "I'll be wearing a black Adidas T-shirt and jeans" no less than three times.

Would he really be wearing that? Could there be more than one man involved? It didn't ring true. Their *Casanova*, as Kat thought of him, would have to be hard-pressed to allow another man in on his scheme, his territory, or his women. But maybe a decoy was exactly what he needed to get away clean.

"Oh, my God, I'm driving myself crazy," she huffed aloud. Checking her makeup in the rearview mirror for the hundredth time, she decided it was as good as it was going to get and got ready to get out of the car.

Looking up, she was stunned immobile as a horde of women crowded around Cross before he'd even stepped onto the patio. The word *dragon* floated through her mind as she watched gorgeous glittering silver scales slide up his arms, disappear under the sleeve his perfectly tight midnight blue T-shirt, and reappear at the nape of his neck.

A shiver skated down her spine and wound around her waist, stopping right on her clit and instantly soaking when he slowly turned his head to the left before staring directly into her eyes. Heat flared to life in his eyes at the same moment the tip of his tongue slid seductively across his bottom lip.

Her body clenched. Her pulse spiked. Her mind filled with images of everything she wanted him to do to her. Forcing her eyes anywhere but at Hunter Cross, Kat took several deep breaths, counted to ten, and with a confidence she didn't feel, got out of the car and headed for the front entrance of Beastly.

Playing the part, she fidgeted with her skirt, touched her earring, and looked from side-to-side several times. Waiting in line, she grinned as Jane's voice whispered in her ear, "Girl, you've got the shy, introvert down to a science. If I didn't know you, I'd swear you were scared outta your skivvies."

"Haven't seen Sway yet," Mitchell, Donovan's new assistant reported. "Cross is on the patio playing his part."

"No shit," Kat swore under her breath.

"Repeat," Mitchell asked. "Unable to copy."

"Nothing," she whispered without moving her lips before stepping forward and letting the big, burly bouncer stamp the back of her hand.

"First time here, darlin'?" His southern twang and the smile that reached his eyes somehow made Kat feel better, like he would do his level best to keep the peace.

"No, I was here the other night for a minute or two."

"Well, you're here during prime hunting time. Can't be shy. The house is packed with regulars." Leaning down, his smile widened as his eyes flashed a brilliant gold and his canines lengthened. "Keep your head up, your eyes open, and holler 'Jake' if you need anything at all."

Patting his think bicep, Kat smiled, "Thanks for the heads up, Jake. I sure will."

Walking away, feeling more confidant with every step, she headed straight for the bar and ordered a margarita on the rocks. Hugging the scratched and sticky wood to keep from being pulled onto the dance floor, she had just picked up her drink when Jane's voice sounded, "A guy fitting Casanova's description is approaching the door."

"Still no eyes on Sway," Mitchell added.

Goose bumps rose all over Kat's body as a low rumble, or maybe it was a growl, immediately followed the assistant analyst's report. Her head automatically whipping toward the patio, once again, she found herself falling into the deep blue depths of Hunter's eyes.

"Abort." His deep baritone made her tremble.

Acting as if she was taking a sip of her drink, Kat hissed, "No."

Ignoring yet another growl, she smoothed the skirt of her dress with her free hand and kept to the plan. Weaving through the gyrating bodies, she carefully picked her way to the last private booth on the left, the booth "Craig" had specifically said would be reserved.

Slowly pulling back the curtain, she slid all

the way in, positioning her back as close to the wall as she could. Remembering every word of her training, she replayed what she'd seen, making mental notes of the subtle changes from the first time she'd been in the nightclub.

Playing up her surprise when Craig's face appeared through the drape, Kat immediately cataloged the differences between the man scooting into the booth with her and the picture she'd seen on the computer screen. There was no doubt in her mind that he was wearing makeup to change the contour of his cheekbones and nose, and he'd colored his hair.

"You really do like margaritas." His voice was too peppy and his smile too bright as he kept going. "You have to be the first honest person I've met since trying out this whole online dating thing."

"I know what you mean."

"Yeah?" He took a long draw of his beer, his eyes stayed glued to hers the entire time. Setting the bottle on the table then his elbows, he steepled his fingers in front of his mouth and coaxed, "Tell me about the weirdest date you've ever been on."

"One time," she batted her eyes and added a nervous giggle. "I reached for the salt and lit the sleeve of my dress on fire."

"No way," he guffawed. "What did the guy

do?"

"Well, that's the funniest part. Neither one of us realized what was happening until the waiter came running over and threw a wet towel on my arm."

"Oh, my God. You had to have been so embarrassed."

"Yeah, I was." She wanted to say *no shit, asshole. And, oh, by the way, I'm making up every word of this bullshit* but instead, she covered her face with both hands and timidly simpered, "The worst part was that while I was in the bathroom trying to clean up, he left and without paying the bill."

Dropping her hands, the second his fingertips touched her wrist, Kat gasped when he deepened his voice and while trying to act suave, clumsily flirted, "I would never do that to someone as beautiful as you."

"Oh no, he didn't," Donovan snorted into her ear. "There is no way this guy can be..."

Whatever the analyst was going to say was cut off as the ear-splitting shriek of a completely freaked out woman cut through the roar of the club. "She's dead! She's dead! Oh, my God, she's dead!"

ELEVEN

Shedding his many admirers like a nasty, lingering case of the clap, Cross sprinted through the club straight toward Kat. Catching sight of her long chocolate- brown locks, he snarled into his mic, "Stay where you are. Keep your cover."

Zig-zagging through the pile-up of drunk lookie-loos, he was just ready to flash his badge and throw the part he was playing in the shitter when a bouncer, who also happen to be an absolutely huge bear shifter, cleared the way. Recognizing the man as a retired cop he'd worked with years ago, Hunter gave the big man a nod of thanks before stopping in the doorway and taking in the scene.

Obviously staged, the corpse was sitting on the marble counter between the sinks like she was awaiting the photographer for her photo shoot. Dressed as a sexy cat, faux-fur leopard ears on a headband and all, her legs were crossed, and her hands laying one atop the other on her knee. Impeccable makeup with lips a fiery red, her heavily mascaraed eyes were eerily open and staring right at the door.

"No wonder the woman was screamin' her fool head off," he muttered to himself.

"Whatcha see, Cross?" Donovan's tone was short and clipped. "I've got CSU on the way. The local cops will be here in less than three minutes. Anything you can give me before they fuck it all up could help."

Inhaling deeply, Hunter let his eyes slide shut as the magic of his dragon sought out anything that didn't belong. Creeping along the floors, up the walls, and into every crevice no matter how small, one thing became glaringly obvious, one man had been in the women's lavatory and his name was Sway.

Unable to comprehend why the absent agent's scent would be permeating every surface of the ladies' restroom, Hunter dug deeper. There it was, just under the surface, the foul stench of rancid blood and rotting flesh, and further under that the faint odor of cheap cleaning fluids.

"I can tell you the owners of this place don't clean," he grunted, still trying to work out what about Sway's scent seemed off. "There's no doubt this is Angela Thomas. She's been cleaned with bleach and made up to look like it's Halloween."

"Shoot me some pics."

Taking out his phone, he stepped to the center of the room and began snapping while also sending real time video. Slowly turning a complete circle, he then went to each of the four stalls and did the same. Finally, he approached the corpse.

Letting the words of his clan, the Rite of the Passage for the Dead, flow through his mind in respect for the woman who'd lost her life, he took pictures from every angle. Getting as close as he could without leaving any evidence that he'd been there, it was the shots of the puncture marks on her neck and wrists that bothered him the most. Lifting the short leopard-print skirt, the same marks were on her inner thighs.

Moving back, he advised, "Photos on the way. Looks like an overzealous vamp kill, or more to the point, someone wants us to *think* a vampire got too frisky with his dinner. See what you think, but in my opinion, those are the smallest fang marks in history."

"You've got about ninety seconds before company finds you mucking about," Donovan warned before changing her tone. "Oh fuck, I see what you mean. I'd bet a Benjamin those are needle marks."

"Then why are they sitting at all the vamp hotspots?" Pausing then immediately deciding he was done covering for the Ken doll, Cross added, "Sway's been in here. This room is lousy with the scent of pretty boy asshole."

"Well, shit, don't hold back, Cross. Tell me how you really feel," Donovan chuckled. "What about your girl?"

"Who?" he spat, playing stupid even though he knew damned good and well who the tech guru was talking about.

"Okay, let's play this game while you're getting the hell outta there before you get caught." Giving a heavy sigh, Donovan asked, "How's Mejia? Cover blown?"

Walking past the bear shifter, Cross whispered, "Thanks. I owe ya." Looking to the side, he was instantly pissed to find Kat being comforted by Craig. Doing everything in his considerable power to keep from sounding like a jealous asshole, he matter-of-factly stated, "Cover looks good."

"Good news that she's okay and her cover's intact. Bad news that there's no way Craig can be our guy," Donovan responded. "And about the whole Sway thing, don't bite my head off, but you know I have to ask… are you sure?"

"Yes," he growled then immediately added in a softer tone, "but something about it was off. Are our crime scene techs going in?"

"Sure are," she answered. "I got to them quick enough and sent the others to a fire somewhere in town."

"Then I'm gonna want to go through all the samples before too many gloves, hands, bags, and chemicals screw with the scents."

"You think you might be wrong?"

"No, I know what I smelled. I'm just wondering how it got there when golden boy is nowhere to be found."

"Good point, but he was there with Kat earlier this week," Donovan murmured.

"Yeah, and he wouldn't have followed her to the bathroom, or taken the chance of a quickie with Mejia along."

"True," she quickly agreed. "Want me to call the boss."

"Not until I've had a chance to go over everything CSU collects. And I'm gonna need you to make the official request since…"

"Since you don't officially exist to anybody but us."

"Well, aren't you a special little star?" Hunter snickered.

"In ways you can only imagine, Cross," Donovan chuckled. "Now, go hide in the fields or whatever it is you do when no one can find you. Four more cars filled with the local boys in blue just pulled up out front."

Wanting to ask if she was going to pull Kat out or let the original scenario play out, Hunter glanced over his shoulder just in time to see Craig going in to lay a kiss on Mejia. Spinning on his heels, he'd stormed halfway across the still-crowded room before Kat's eyes met his with a look that pled, *Please don't fuck this up for me.*

Making himself stop just as a voice over the speaker system announced that the bar was closed, and non-alcoholic drinks would be free while the police detained everyone for questioning, Hunter did another one-eighty, and disappeared into the crowd. Out onto the patio then straight into the darkness, he found himself walking the rows of a cornfield exactly the way Donovan had suggested.

Angry that she'd switched off his earbud, but knowing it was so no one knew he was there, Hunter carefully watched the scene as he waited for hours. Finally, when the first rays of the sun turned the horizon light blue and pink, he caught a glimpse of Kat walking to her car.

Irritated with himself for being relieved that she was alone, he couldn't help but keep his eyes glued to his mate until she drove away. It was another hour and a half before the last of the patrons had been dismissed and still almost two more hours before the Nokesville Police and FBI CSU packed up and left.

Slipping through the employee entrance at the back of the building, Hunter went straight to the ladies' room. He had to see if Sway's scent was still there. It was driving him crazy that he couldn't pinpoint what about it had his preternatural senses in a tizzy.

Littered with baggies, wrappers, and bright yellow cardboard numbers from the Crime Scene Unit, the bathroom looked totally different with the debris scattered about and the absence of Angela's corpse. Blocking out the scent of gallons of luminol, fingerprint powder, and latex, he focused on the glowing trail of dragon mixed with panther.

Deliberately walking the same path the Ken doll had, Hunter found himself running straight into the back wall of the last stall. Not stopping there, but literally running into it like Sway had slipped through the concrete and brick. Refusing to breathe in the noxious fumes of cleaning supplies and human filth as he knelt and looked behind the tank, the dragon cursed, "Well, fuck me."

Reaching behind him, he tore a small piece

of toilet paper from the roll then carefully used it to retrieve a tiny piece of evidence all the others had missed. Wrapping it tightly, he shoved it into his pocket before pushing to his feet.

Leaving the club the same way he snuck in, Hunter casually walked to his Harley, ready with an excuse should anyone stop him. When no one did, he scanned the area one more time just to be sure before pulling his phone from his pocket and powering it on.

Listening as it rang, he just about to disconnect when Donovan answered, "Jane's Bar and Grill. You kill 'em. We grill 'em. Whatcha need, Hunter?"

TWELVE

Tossing and turning, pacing the floors, and checking her phone every two minutes was driving her crazy. Patience was not a virtue she possessed, nor was it one she aspired to have. Kat was an achiever, and God help anyone who got in her way...except for the boss.

On her way to the office, needing to see what evidence, if any was gathered at Beastly and to confirm her suspicion that Angela had died from an uncontrolled asthma attack, she'd gotten the call every agent hated. The one from Brock ordering her to maintain cover and use the closest safe house just in case she was being followed.

Politely accepting her orders, she double checked to be sure her phone was off before throwing the device on the seat of her company-borrowed car and cursing in a mix of Spanish,

English in what her uncle called Spanglish. Furious and frustrated, she'd bitched aloud the entire way to the house, up the walk, and into the kitchen at the back.

Not only was she in a strange place without any of her own stuff, but she was pissed at being cut out of her own case. It didn't matter that Brock was right, that everyone had to play it safe until they knew for sure what had happened to their victim and how the perp got her into Beastly. She had a right to be at the office just as much as any other agent...*more* in her opinion.

Picking up the phone for the hundredth time, her finger hovered over a single name in her contacts. Someone she knew would have the answers she needed. An agent who seemed to have *all* the answers about damn near everything.

No, she shouldn't call him. They were hardly friends. He pissed her off with his arrogant attitude and high-handed actions, but the fact remained that her nerves were rattled, and he was the only one she wanted to talk to. The only friggin' name that came to mind.

"You're losing your damned mind, Katrina Andrea. He'll make you feel stupid. Treat you like you're an idiot. Make jokes at your expense. Or worse, he won't answer and laugh about the fact that you took the time to call." Making another lap around the living room, she mused, "But then again, maybe he wouldn't. Maybe he'd see it as initiative. As taking charge. As tenacity. As doing whatever it took to get the bad guy and close the case."

Falling back onto the couch, she crossed her arms, uncrossed her arms, looked at her phone, pulled her legs up under her, and finally huffed, "And there really is a land with little people, a talking lion, tin man, scarecrow, and a chick that can click her heels and go home. I've lost my fucking mind."

Grabbing the remote, she turned on the TV. Flipping through the hundred fifty-some channels without really looking at the screen, she continued to go over everything she knew about Craig.

Yes, he *had* been wearing makeup, but it turned out he had a raging case of acne. His name really was Craig Nielson. He really did live on Woodward Ave. And he *was* thirty-one years old. There were no doubts. The dweeb had shown her his license in an effort to make her trust him enough to say yes to a second date.

Of course, she had agreed with a big sappy smile and a flutter of her lashes, and *of course*, she was going to call and cancel because…*why bother*? He wasn't Casanova. She wasn't attracted to him in the slightest. And more to the point, he wasn't Hunter Cross.

Groaning aloud as she let her head fall backward, Kat grumbled, "What the hell is wrong with me? Hunter Cross is a jerk. He makes me want to rip my hair out." Grinding her teeth, she growled, "And rip his clothes off, and kiss every inch of that amazing body, and beg him to do the same to me."

Springing off the couch and pacing the floors for the hundredth time, she kept ranting, "I would lick him like an all-day sucker and then some. He is the one man I would literally tie to the bed so he could never leave. I would..."

The chiming of her phone blessedly cut off her rant. Snatching it from where she'd dropped it on the couch, absolutely sure that Jane was finally calling her with an update, Kat stopped and stared. It was a number she didn't know. One no one would know because it was only five digits.

Gawking at a phone that was no longer ringing, she headed for the encrypted laptop in the tiny office. Her fingers had just touched the cool metal lid when the same number reappeared on the screen.

Without time to access the FBI database, she swiped the screen and lifted the device to her ear. Before she could answer, the sound of an antique music box, its pins dragging across the cylinder and scratching the teeth of the comb filled the room. It was a tune she knew by heart, one that took her all the way back to the little yellow cottage just outside Mexico City where she'd grown up.

"Who is this?" she demanded. "How did you get this number?"

"K-Kat," a hoarse croak she knew she should recognize pleaded. "K-Kat, you have to..." Stopped by a deep, rattling cough that trailed off into sounds of retching, the voice finally returned wheezing, "Run, Kat, ru..."

"Wait! Wait! Who is this?"

A stab to the side of her neck left Kat spinning to the left before stumbling toward the couch. Missing the mark and falling to her knees right beside it, she lurched forward. The biting scent of rubbing alcohol, the cloyingly sweet tang of rotting fruit, and a spicy whiff of frankincense stung her already blurry eyes as she struggled to stay upright.

Grabbing at a shadow, she felt the cold bite of steel immediately before the all-too-familiar sound of handcuffs snapping shut echoed in her ears. Fighting to stay conscious, she collapsed backward.

Scooped up by a pair of large arms, her limp body refused to respond as her vision narrowed to a single dot of dank, yellow light. Opening her mouth, she simply couldn't get the words to form.

Flailing her head backward, giving one last try at escape, her captor whispered, "It's no use, Katrina. Now, you're mine."

THIRTEEN

"How much longer?"

"Two minutes less than the last time you asked," Donovan groused, not looking up from the screen of her laptop. "They said an hour. It'll be an hour. Stop pacing. Go get coffee. Run around the block. Play in traffic. Hell, go mess up Brock's desk, just let me get this request done or you'll never get the rest of the evidence from Beastly."

"But…"

"But nothing. The lab is analyzing that sliver of silver. You already know it had blood on it and that it was Sway's. I'm not sure what you think they can find that your senses don't already know, but you insisted and I did as you asked. So, now we wait."

"I told you why I wanted them to test it," he growled. "There is something weird about the way it smells. It's Sway, but then there's something about it that's not Sway. I can't explain it."

"Right."

"Okay, hotshot. How do you explain his trail ending at a wall? And, before you ask, no, that's not where it started. Actually, it's where it stopped only because I can't walk through walls."

"And here I thought you were Super Agent man."

Ignoring Donovan, needing to say it all out loud one more time, Hunter continued, "And Sway can't walk through walls either. No matter what you all think. But disappearing into the wall isn't the weirdest thing..."

"You don't say?" Jane grumbled.

"...it mysteriously moved without a trail. Like jumped ten feet, didn't touch anything and bingo-bango reappeared in the center of a stall."

"Bingo-bango? That's a new one."

"Don't sass me, Donovan," Hunter gave up and acknowledged her running commentary, but refused to stop his own. "There was no backtracking, no layers, *nada*. Ken doll stench was there, it was gone, and then it was over there. And this bears repeating, Sway may be picture perfect, but the bastard can't walk through walls or do fucking magic tricks."

"Damn straight," Ramirez chimed in, entering the tech room. "He's not fucking perfect either," he added, heading straight for his wife.

Turning away as the happy couple said a *very* thorough hello, Hunter couldn't stop thinking about Kat. Sure, the boss had told her not to come into the office and had tucked her away in a safe house. It just wasn't like his tenacious mate not to find a way to call in and talk to Donovan about the case.

When an hour went by without word from Mejia, he'd called the undercover officers stationed outside her location. Douglas reported everything was okay. Nothing out of the ordinary. So why was his dragon charging the confines of his mind, pummeling Hunter to be let free, to protect Katrina.

"You can turn around now," Donovan laughed. "We should be good for another ten minutes or so."

"Make that five," Ramirez grinned while waggling his eyebrows.

"I've got an email," Donavan announced before Cross could make a smartass comment.

Across the room and peering over her shoulder as fast as his feet would carry him, Cross read the findings twice before shaking his head and thinking aloud, "It's his. They say it's a ninety-nine-point-nine percent match to the sample you gave them."

"Did they test for any chemical presence?" Ramirez quizzed.

"Wouldn't matter. It's his blood." Rolling his shoulders to relieve some of the tension, Hunter sighed, "I gotta go tell the boss. I'm already gonna lose my ass for waiting this long. I just thought…"

His words trailing off as the phone on Donovan's desk rang, he opened the door when she gasped, "Say that again."

Stopping in his tracks, Hunter heard four words that made his blood run cold. "Agent Mejia is missing."

Back across the room with his hand reaching for the receiver, he slammed the hard plastic to his ear and roared, "How long since last contact?"

"Ten minutes."

"Visual?"

"No, sir. Text."

"FUCK! What the fuck?!" Pulling the phone from his ear then pushing it right back into place, he snarled, "Could you be any fucking stupider? When was the last visual contact?"

"Nine a.m."

Eyes flying to the clock on the wall, he bellowed, "Three-and-a-half-fucking hours ago? Fucking morons! Stupid fucking mor..."

"What is going on in here?" Brock's boomed as he threw the door open.

Slamming the receiver on the desk next to Donovan, Hunter spun toward the boss, crossed the room in two huge strides, and stopping just short of bumping Brock's nose with his own, roared, "The bastard's got Kat."

FOURTEEN

She regained consciousness a bit and took a moment to study her body and surroundings. Hot and humid, miserably sticky, the air so thick it was hard to draw a breath… Covering in slimy sweat, her clothes clung to her skin like heavy strips of papier-mâché…

Had the air conditioner broken? What was going on? Climate change was real, but this shit was ridiculous. It hadn't been hot when she'd gotten home. Was the AC even on? What time was it? What day was it? What was that horrible smell?

Whatever was happening, she'd have to get up and call her landlord before she melted into a puddle of slushy Latin goo. She was hotter than she could ever remember being, and she grew up south of the border.

No way she could deal with being miserable all the time. Being hot just sucked. There were only so many clothes she could take off before *ta-da* she would be down to her birthday suit. God knew the rent was high enough. "Premium rent for premium location," the landlord had touted. Well, dammit all to hell, everything in the "premium place" should work.

"Maybe later..." she mumbled aloud. "Need...sleep..."

Foggy, lost in her own mind, she was more unconscious than actually asleep, swimming against a mental tide of steamy, gooey quicksand. Thick, unbreakable, steel bands tightened around her chest...or was there a huge rock pressing the life out of her? Was this what happened when somebody got too hot? Was this heat exhaustion? A heat stroke? Maybe she was just dreaming...

NO! Wake up, Kat! Wake your ass up, NOW!

Was she yelling at herself? Could that happen? Why would she do that? The alarm hadn't gone off, she wasn't late for work...or was she? Nothing made sense. Everything was upside-down and inside-out.

Wait... No, she wasn't the one screaming, *was she*? It was inside her mind. So, it was her...kinda, in a manner of speaking. That little voice her *abuela* said would keep her safe, always be there to warn her away from danger. But why now? What the hell could go wrong in her own bed?

Fighting to open her eyes, trying to swallow with her tongue stuck against the roof of her mouth and her throat as dry as the Sahara, the icy claws of dread sunk their jagged tips into her psyche. Cold, shocking, dangerously alarming, an explosion of adrenalin shot through her body.

Jerking her hands from over her head, pure agony exploded in her wrists as the clang of metal against metal echoed through her mind at the same time it bit into her flesh. Something was wrong...*really, really wrong*. She was caught, shackled, couldn't move. Inhaling deeply through her mouth, she gagged and coughed and struggled to catch her breath as acrid fumes of rotting vegetation and decaying fish wound into a suffocating ball in the base of her throat.

Forcing her eyelids open, she shook with a volatile tincture of fear and rage when she could see no farther than the tip of her nose. Matted, tangled, and slick with mud, her hair was thrown over her face, so heavy she couldn't move it no matter what she tried.

Rushing toward complete consciousness, flashes of lights, blurry pictures, misshapen faces, all flooded her mind. It was maddening frenzy she couldn't comprehend and couldn't make stop.

Holding tightly to the tiny bits of reality she could pluck from the miasma, her nails bit into her palms, the pain dredging her from the murderous undertow of the narcotics swimming through her veins. Working backward and without concentrating on one thing for longer than a split second, the pieces of the jigsaw puzzle her memories had become blessedly began to fall into place.

Huge holes, missing shards with no border, some bits too were bright, others too dark, and still another set so far out of focus she let them fall away. Turning her head sideways to escape the stench of the muck in her hair, she gasped at the thimbleful of almost fresh air. Her neck ached, a concentrated pang just like a Band-Aid bring ripped off before she was ready radiated from one small spot.

And there it was... She *had* been drugged. Injected with something incredibly fasting acting. Visions where she was falling forward and the thud of her knees slamming into a tile floor burst into view. A horrible floral-patterned couch pulsed in and out of focus. "Where the hell am I... *the safe house,*" she silently swore.

That was the spark, the nudge her brain needed to replay everything in painfully specific detail. She'd been kidnapped...by someone who knew where she was...knew how to get into the back entrance of the safe house...*knew her by name.*

It was time to get to work. Time to figure out where she was, who had done this to her, and how she was going to escape. Slamming her eyes as tight as they would go, she did the only thing that made sense, she focused on identifying the sounds around her.

A *whoosh-whoosh-whoosh* on her left was closer than the *drip-drip-drip* somewhere behind her head but not as close as the *clickclick-clickclick-clickclick* just beyond the tip of her toes. She was in a large exposed space where the left side was open to the outside if the smells assaulting her nose meant anything at all.

"Put it together, Kat. Pull that shit outta thin air like they taught you to do. You scored the highest in your class. Think. *Think, dammit.* You have to figure out where you are if you're gonna get out of this alive," she fumed under her breath.

Squeezing her eyes tighter, this time she held her breath, directing all her energy on the *whoosh*. This wasn't the first time she'd heard that noise. It was too familiar not to have been in the last year or so. But where? She'd been so many places. Only paying attention when it was for work or part of her training.

Starting soft, it got louder and louder crescendoing to a pinnacle then faded out again the entire time its mechanical cadence was somehow out of time. Rotating! It was rotating 180 degrees one way and then back, over and over.

"A fan. It's fan. Not a little house fan. An industrial fan," she thought aloud. "Yes! Got it."

But not in a factory. Wherever she was simply wasn't that big. There would've been more echoes, more dust, less air and the smells would've been musty not moldy. So, not at the old industrial park or the condemned tenements on the eastside. Knowing what something wasn't meant she was one step closer to knowing what it was. At least that's what one of her instructors at the academy always said.

Turning her attention to the drip that remained constant with a bit of a warble from one to the other. It had to be water, or even raindrops, falling onto a tarp or into a shallow plastic bucket...*probably*. It was the only thing that fit but did that go with the fan?

Shaking with frustration, knowing she was taking too long, sure her captor would be back, Kat prayed for something...*anything* new. Whipping her head to the other side, she scooted and pushed the scant inches she could until just the tip of her nose finally pushed through her hair.

No smell of salt water, no sound of boat engines, no horns, she couldn't be at the docks or anywhere close. If nothing else, she would be able to hear the waves splashing against the cement pylons holding up the wharves.

There was no giving up. She *would* figure it out. No stupid fucker who had to drug his victims was going to get the best of her. She just needed to think, to get her heart to stop pounding and her imagination to stop coming up with one morbid situation after another.

Flipping her head back the other way, she stopped cold and refused to breathe. "Whispers. Somebody's here." Holding perfectly still, she willed the faint, murmurs to her ears.

Ragged coughing and dry-heaving, followed by gut-wrenching gagging then another round of coughing interrupted the hums. The guy was either gonna hurl, die, or both, and she couldn't let that happen.

Ready to come to the ailing person's aid, the blood froze in her veins as the same raspy voice that had whispered in her ear, snarled, "You're a weak fuck, and weak fucks are expendable."

Waiting for more, sure it was coming, a shocked scream flew from her lips when a huge hand gripped the hair hiding her face, jerking straight toward the ceiling. Her shoulders popped out their sockets and her neck was craned at an odd angle, but she refused to cry out more than she already had.

Shifting her eyes left, right, up, and down, trying to catch a glimpse of her abductor, hot fetid breath hit the side of her neck as the bastard licked her cheek and sneered, "You taste good enough to eat."

FIFTEEN

Pushing past Brock, Hunter made it halfway down the hall before the boss was standing in front of him with a look of murder in his eyes. "How the hell?" Unwilling to wait for the answer or even slow down, he swerved to the left only to be snared as a thick veil of magic fell all around him.

Unable to move, stuck in place, he shifted his eyes as far right as they would go and watched Brock deliberately closing the distance between them. Leaning close, the boss warned, "Pull that shit again and I'll bury you so deep, the fucking Devil won't be able to find you."

Just as quickly as he'd been caught, Hunter was released from whatever voodoo the boss had used. A million questions ran through his mind, questions he'd ask after Kat was safe and Sway was dead.

"My office," Brock spat, walking away with the arrogance of a man who knew his order would be followed.

"I've gotta go," Hunter contradicted. "We can have a tea party later."

"Cross."

The threat was clear. Hunter didn't care.

"Brock. You want answers. You better catch up."

With every step, he waited to be stricken with whatever super power the boss had running through his veins. So, when Brock appeared at Hunter's side as he was racing down the stairs, the dragon was more than a little relieved.

Barely touching the floor as he flew out the door, Hunter turned right as Brock snarled, "My car. I don't ride bitch."

Deciding he'd pushed his luck as far as he could, Hunter spun around, caught up and was in the car a second after the locks were disengaged. "Drive it like you stole it," he growled, thankful when Brock left rubber on the asphalt and rode on two wheels when he turned out of the parking lot.

Never one to mince words, Hunter demanded, "What the fuck were you thinking letting Sway anywhere near Kat?"

"I was thinking that you're too much of an asshole. That you knew she was your mate and weren't going to do anything about it. That you'd let testosterone and pride get in the way of the investigation and put a new agent in danger. That at least if Mejia was partnered with Sway you'd focus on the case if it meant keeping her safe." Sliding his eyes to the side and glaring as he made a quick left, he spat, "Anymore stupid questions?"

"Did you know he was dirty?"

"Do you know for sure he is?"

Leaving a perfect imprint of his knuckles as he slammed his fist into the dashboard, Hunter roared, "Fuck yes, I do!" Hitting the wounded plastic again and again, the accusation flew like flames. "And so do you. Do you need a two-by-four to the fucking head?"

Another right and an immediate left then straight into a driveway before standing on the brakes, Brock slammed the car into park and opened his door. Out of the car and halfway to the porch before Hunter caught up with him, the boss clipped, "You have your doubts, or you would've already brought everything to me."

"Donovan," Hunter spat, lifting his foot and kicking in the door to Sway's house. "She was talking to you the whole damned time."

"What of it?"

Ignoring the question in favor of finding any information leading to the location of his mate, Hunter went straight to the back of the house and into the tiny office. Ripping open drawers, tearing through files, throwing papers that didn't suit his search over his shoulder, his hand wrapped around the handle of the bottom drawer of the desk and pulled. "Locked! Fuck that!"

Tearing it completely out into the light of day, he let the broken wood fall onto the floor, retrieving the olive-green, metal lockbox as it flew through the air. Breaking the lock, he snatched out an envelope of photos and another full of folded papers.

Shredding the wrapper with the tips of his talons as they pushed through the ends of his fingers, he boomed, "Got him!"

Appearing at the door, Brock demanded, "What did you find?"

Grabbing the pictures and the documents, Hunter sprinted around the desk and past the boss as he snarled, "Tell ya in the car."

Leaving the door hanging on one hinge with Brock at his back, Hunter jumped from the porch, hit the ground running, and slid across the hood of the car. Any other time, he would've had a smartass comment about Starsky and Hutch, but in this case, all he wanted was to find Kat. She was all that mattered.

Bang! Bang! Two doors shut. Key went into the ignition. Engine gunned. And they were off.

"Tell me," Brock barked.

"Sway's got pictures of this old greenhouse on the other side of Nokesville." He threw the photos on the seat. "The route from here to there is perfectly documented. Deed transfer from Emmett Smith to Wyatt Sway, title of ownership in the name of Wyatt Sway, and receipt of cash transfer from the account name of Wyatt Sway to the out-of-state account of Emmett Smith." Slamming the documents on top of the photos, he snidely asked, "Is the Ken doll a closet florist?"

"How the fuck would I know?" Steering the racing car under the I95 overpass then onto Aden Road, he goaded, "But I'll ask him as soon as I see him."

"Not if I get to him first. I'm gonna—"

"Not do a fucking thing but get Kat out safely and let me handle *my* agent."

"What the fuck is wrong with you, Brock? The kid got pictures of you fucking a goat? He knows you wear lady's silky skivvies? Stop protecting the piece of shit."

"I'm gonna let that one go," Brock growled.

"I know you're freaked the hell out and ready to go scaly on me, but never forget, piss me off and I'll drop you where you sit."

Refusing to admit the boss was right even as the scales of his dragon covered the back of his hands and climbed his arms, Hunter stared out the windshield. The evidence was right there. Sway was dirty. He'd taken Kat. Brock may be the boss and have seriously funky magic that could most likely turn him and his dragon inside out, but that fucking bastard pretty boy was gonna pay for laying a finger on his mate.

Listening as Brock called in backup, wondering if that was for Sway's benefit or Kat's, Hunter grabbed the door handle and sprang from the car at the exact second the boss slowed at the turn into the lane to the greenhouse.

"Cross! Cross? You stupid mother fucker! You're gonna get her killed!"

The boss's rage was a living, breathing entity that Hunter had no doubt would strike him dead. Ducking into the overgrown vacant lot adjacent to Sway's hothouse, the dragon sprinted along the property line. Winding around stacks of rusted barrels, piles of rotting pallets, and mountains of black plastic pots, he used everything he could for cover.

Wrapping himself in the cover of his dragon's magic to avoid signaling Sway that he was near, Hunter stopped at the far side of the last remaining greenhouse when the scent of Kat's blood punched him in the face.

Experience battled with instinct. His dragon roared, *"GO SAVE KAT!"* Everything he'd learned as an agent argued, *"Get a better look or you'll be the reason she dies."*

Ramming his dragon behind a heavy wall of willpower and mysticism, Hunter inched closer. Pushing his preternatural senses farther with every step, he let out the breath he'd been holding when his heart sped forward, stuttered, stopped and then fell into perfect sync with the healthy beat of Kat's. She was alive and almost as pissed off as he was which meant they had a better than good chance of making it out alive. Mad trumped scared all day, every day.

Searching the rest of the building, he found ten other steady heartbeats forty yards away. Thankfully, the rest of the girls who'd been abducted were still alive, bleeding, but alive.

Still looking for Sway, he was just about to give up, go after his mate, and deal with whatever he found when several things became glaringly clear. Not one, but *two* shifters were in that fucking deathtrap greenhouse. One was standing. One was on the floor and barely breathing. Both were people Hunter knew.

SIXTEEN

Definitely tired of being drugged. Sick of being treated like a Stretch Armstrong doll. So over waking up in the dark with her hair matted to her face, Kat gave up being scared or trying to figure out where she was and growled, "Look, I don't give a shit what you look like, but if you don't get this fucking hair outta my face, I'm going to suffocate."

Hurried footfalls raced across the room right before a heavy hand she knew all too well wrapped around her hair and ripped it from her face. Stopping only when her neck was pulled back as far as it could possibly go and she was staring at…well, she had no idea, did the asshole snarl, "Now, shut the fuck up, bitch."

"D-do as he-he s-says, Kat." The words had barely been stuttered before once again the person sounded as if he was going to cough up a lung.

Ignoring the pain slicing through her neck and shoulders, slashing down her spine and setting off a fiery relay of twinges and pinches in her ass, Kat's eyes followed the gagging. Gasping when she saw a bloody, beaten, and literally gray-skinned Sway, she gulped, "Sway. Oh, my God, what have they—" *SLAP!*

Backhanded before she could finish her sentence, she disregarded the burning agony in her cheek and whipped her head to the side. Finding a masked man wearing a black hoodie and faded jeans, something within her snapped.

Laughing out loud, she guffawed, "Holy shit! I've been kidnapped by a wannabe thug!"

Dropping her chin, she felt a whoosh of air from her captor's fist as it flew past her ear. Throwing her head backward, she outsmarted the asshole again this time taunting, "Dude, you suck at this game."

For the third time, his ham-fisted fingers dug into her hair, jerking her head back with such force that the bones in her neck snapped and she couldn't catch her breath. Manically laughing as he punched her face over and over, Kat was just about to pass out when Sway's horrified roar cut through her delirium.

"She said you could not kill Kat until Cross was here."

Time stood still. Opening one eye because the other refused to budge, she saw a meaty fist hovering inches from her nose. The ragged breathing of her attacker let her know he was deep in an internal debate. The little voice in the back of her head was telling her to keep her mouth shut, but Kat was over all the bullshit.

"Go ahead," she lisped through broken and missing teeth. "Beat my brains out. You know you want to." Sucking air past her bloody, swollen lips, she rasped, "Show that bitch who's boss."

Letting go of her hair with such vehemence that her head bounced against the chair she was tied to, the masked man stomped away. A fist hitting something wooden proceeded the slamming of a door before she heard the hard soles of shoes crunching over gravel.

Head listing to the side, she caught a glimpse of Sway. Bad didn't begin to describe how he looked. Not only was his skin the color of gunmetal but upon her closer, one-eyed inspection, she saw thin black lines snaking their way across his face and down his arms.

"You okay, Sway?" Sure, it was a stupid thing to ask but it was all her scrambled brains could come up with, and it worked.

The sick sound of a watery, snickering cough bubbled up and out of the agent's dry and cracked lips before he croaked, "Just peachy." More coughing and gagging then a stuttered "Y-you?"

"Never better." Dots of bright white light chased bigger blobs of black and gray across her vision. "I think I'm gonna pass out though."

"Stay a-awake, Kat," Sway stammered. "You have t-to st-stay awake."

Fighting a wave of nausea, Kat rolled her head to the side and promptly threw up down her own arm. Spitting the bile as best she could with her lips swelling more with every beat of her heart, she rasped, "I think my arm's broken."

"Dislocated," Sway hacked.

"Both?" Trying to get her head, now heavier than a bowling ball and pounding like a jackhammer, to roll to the other side, she gave up and asked, "Are they both dislocated?"

When no answer came, Kat doubled her efforts to get her head to move. Completely numb, only the throbbing of her face and the thumping in her head reminding her that she was still alive, she had to know how bad it was. It was the only hope she had of escaping.

Counting down in her head, preparing for what she was sure was going to be the most excruciating pain she'd ever experienced, Kat never got to make a move. Stopped before she got started by the mocking sound of a slow clap and the unmistakable click of stiletto heels on concrete, she did the only thing she could think of…she was a smart ass.

"Lookie there, Sway. We've got an audience."

SEVENTEEN

The blaring of sirens was getting closer and Brock was bearing down on him. In minutes, the entire place would be a mass of agents, officers, and SWAT teams, all with rules, regulations and protocols he had no fucking time for. Kat was in that building. Her life was in danger. There was only one choice he could make. Hunter had to save his mate.

Sprinting to the opposite side of the building, his heart stopped dead as the sound of fist thrashing flesh reached his ears. Tearing around the corner, the renewed scent of Kat's blood had his dragon shredding Hunter's mental containment and thrashing against the underside of his skin.

Dashing through a huge hole in the concrete wall, he raced toward the beat of his mate's heart...then he heard her voice. Strength filled every syllable. Forté that rivaled his own simply refused to be beaten. She was a warrior, absolutely no doubt about it.

He could scent her fear, but she refused to let it win. Katrina Mejia was resilient. She was smarter than a whip. She was the most beautiful woman he'd ever laid eyes on. And fuck it all, she was his.

Running headlong into the room, eyes on his mate, Cross slid to stop when an old and haunting voice purred, "I thought they were lying, but it seems they were right. This waste of skin and bones really is your mate. Oh, Hunter, darling, a measly human blood bag? How could fate be so cruel? Good thing I'm here to save you."

Staring at Kat, cataloging her injuries and knowing she wouldn't last long, he poured the unyielding healing magic of his dragon through the bond rapidly forming from his soul to hers. Shocked at how natural it felt, not wanting to admit to himself that he was becoming truly whole for the first time in his incredibly long life, Hunter promised her with his eyes to bring an end to her suffering. Slowly shifting his entire body toward an abomination from his past, he focused on defeating an old nemesis.

Body wound tightly, his muscles vibrated with the need to exact revenge. Hate festered and boiled, feeding his desire to rip the woman apart… the *thing* standing before him limb from limb.

"Greta," he forced the words through gritted teeth. "I might have known."

"But you didn't, did you?" Crossing her arms across her chest and leaning to the left while throwing her other long, shapely leg to the right, the dhampyre he'd unfortunately left alive a hundred years ago arched an eyebrow as she tsked. "I admit, it disappoints me that I had to go to such lengths to get your attention."

"Well, you did. I'm here. Let Kat go."

Throwing back her head and laughing, her long ebony hair flowing down her back like the ashen waterfall to Hell, Greta's black eyes glowed with malice when she looked back and countered, "But we're just getting to know each other, your little Katrina and me."

"Fuck that," Kat slurred, his heart heavy knowing the pain she must be in as he shoved even more of his innate curative powers into her. "Kill her, Cross. Fucking kill her."

Remembering how very much Greta liked to play games, Hunter made himself relax. He wouldn't save Kat if he acted rashly or let his rage get the best of him.

Spreading his feet shoulder-width apart and

letting his hands fall to his side, he shushed his mate, hoped she knew he was playing a part and nodded to the dhampyre, "And how's that going?"

Holding his breath, barely keeping his dragon from bursting forth, he watched as Greta made a show of approaching his mate and stroking her snarled hair. Wiping her index finger along the gaping wound dissecting Kat's cheek, she flirtatiously slid the digit into her mouth.

Moaning and sucking, rolling her eyes, and slowly moving it in and out across her lips, she sighed in mock ecstasy, "Yes, Hunter, darling, I see why you like her. She's tastes heavenly. Should we share her?"

Spiraling close to the edge, knowing time was almost up as he listened to an entire horde of law enforcement officers descending on the greenhouse, Cross roared, "Stop the fucking game. What do you want?"

Moving so fast, he could barely track her, Hunter was forced to stand helpless as Greta seized Kat from the chair, stripping away the restraints. Her back to the dhampyre's chest, his mate's battered body shook in pain where Greta's arm was wrapped tightly around her bosom.

Jerking Kat's head to the side, the dhampyre ran the sharp tips of her fangs along his mate's hammering jugular as she hissed, "To kill the one you love."

In the blink of an eye everything in Hunter's world switched to slow motion. Kat was the center of his universe. He could see Brock leading a team toward the building. His gaze was captured by the single drop of bright red blood flowing down his mate's porcelain neck. Then he saw the murderous look on Greta's face.

Releasing the iron grip he had on his dragon, Hunter breathed into the instantaneous transformation from man to beast. Trusting in the intuition they shared, he knew his dragon would control the form they took. Moving while his body grew in height and width, he took hold of the massive influx of magic and adrenalin, letting it energize every cell.

Reveling in the feel of silver scales cascading over his elongated limbs, covering his chest, and spilling down his back, he roared in exultation at the raw, unbridled power infusing every fiber of his being. Basking in the sensation of the bulge and flex of his enlarged muscles, the shift into his nine-foot battle dragon ended as quickly as it had begun.

Tossing Kat to the side, she threw her arms open wide. Thankful that a seriously injured Sway had been there to catch his mate, Cross gave a single nod to the furious dhampyre before him.

Fangs extended out of her mouth so far that

the tips pushed against the outer line of her bottom lip. Her nails, now long, jagged talons, he knew were imbued with caustic acid that over time would corrode even his scales. She was the picture of her mother, Lorna. Memories of the vicious battle with the dhampyre leader and her coven swirled through his mind, ending as always with him swinging his sword and beheading her for her crimes.

"A century of waiting," she hissed. "Planning, plotting, keeping track of your whereabouts, knowing your every move before you even made it, and finally revenge shall be mine."

Standing perfectly still, waiting and watching, Hunter unhurriedly raised his arm. Spreading his thick powerful fingers as wide as they would go, he smiled when his talons grew to twice their normal size and the fire of his dragon flared in his veins.

Then a tiny sting on his thigh set his dragon screaming—and then nothing. His animal body deflated into his human form. There was complete silence in his head. What the fuck happened to his dragon?

As he lay on the concrete floor, he reached for something attached to his upper leg. He pulled out a dart.

"What the fuck have you done, Greta?"

She released a heinous laugh. "Testing a new serum," she replied.

His arm felt heavy and it dropped onto the floor. He hated to play her game, but something was happening to him. "What kind of serum, Greta? Tell me."

She gave him a coy look and sashayed toward him. "Oh, you know, something that's been in the works for a long time. Something that takes away your animal and knocks out the human host."

The toe of her high-heel shoe pushed at his arm. She glanced over his naked body, stopping midway down. "I always wondered if dragons were bigger in size *everywhere*. I got my answer. Very nice." She strolled around him. Not even his little finger followed the command his brain gave to move.

An unfamiliar growl came from his mate's way. "Get away from him, bitch," his Kat said. If he didn't know her better, he would've thought she had a shifter in her.

Greta stomped toward Kat and Sway, both weak and stumbling to stand. When close enough, Greta kicked his mate's side, flipping her onto her back.

"Stay out of this. You'll die in a minute," she glanced at him, "after he's placed in the perfect place to watch you slowly suffer."

Rapid gun fire blasted outside. Seemed the good guys and the bad guys had met in a shootout. Question was who would come out on top. Greta hurried to a window and looked out.

Sway lay in a fetal position between Hunter and Kat. His lips mumbled, and Hunter strained to hear his words. Was his dragon really gone?

"She's your mate. Stop being an ass and accept what fate has gifted you, dumbass," Sway said. "Give your power to her."

Of course. Hunter recalled what Sway was talking about. Dragon mates could share certain things through their bond. But he hadn't claimed her, said he didn't want a mate.

Sway was right; he was a dumbass. Having a mate wasn't a prison, a mate was freedom. He'd been so afraid of losing himself, that he'd closed himself to everyone. No one was going to change him, make him do what he didn't want.

Seeing Kat sprawled, unconscious, his heart ached to hold her, to make her better. Only his dragon's magic could heal. Could it help his mate? Maybe, if he got over himself and accepted her.

After taking a deep breath, he opened his heart and let the mate connection sink in. She snapped into his link, now, *their* link. Her pain was his pain. He ached everywhere.

Even though his animal was supposedly gone, he hoped the magic remained. No human created serum could take away magic. Only magic could fight magic.

Focusing his mind on his mate, he sent her his magic along the bond. They hadn't mated fully, but they were intertwined in spirit. After a moment, he saw her hand twitch. She was letting him into her heart and soul, no questions asked. He was truly humbled. The magic was working its. . .magic. Great. Now he was losing his mind on stupid jokes.

Greta's shoes clicked, coming toward him. Shit. There hadn't been enough time. Kat wouldn't be well enough to run.

His shoulders lifted, head falling back, eyes staring into pure evil. Greta gave him an air kiss. "Time for the show to begin, lovey."

The gun battle outside had calmed. He suspected they were in a hostage situation with her men hunkered down inside, waiting for orders.

She dropped him sitting up against a steel support beam facing where Kat and Sway lay. Only his eyes moved. Greta squatted close to his head and ran her tongue along his lips. Her teeth bit, stinging as she licked his blood.

Her hand slid down his leg and grabbed his exposed cock. "Tell me, Hunter, what is the best way to get most of your blood in one place for a delicious meal?" Her hand fisted around his dick and stroked. With a growl, he realized he had no control over his body. Not even able to keep his erection down.

He felt his blood rushing to the center of his groin in reaction to the unwanted stimulus. She flicked her elongated teeth with her tongue. "This will be so tasty." She leaned forward onto her knees, bending over, mouth open. He closed his eyes. If he could throw up, he would.

His senses picked up on his mate's scent. He popped his eyes wide to see his love standing behind Greta, wooden chair she was once tied to raised over her head.

"I said, stay away from him." The chair whipped through the air, smashing into the dhampyre's back, knocking the bitch away from him. The chair splintered into pieces. His mate was freakin' strong.

In a heartbeat, Greta was on her feet, hands around Kat's neck. His mate crossed her bleeding wrists and grabbed the arms extended toward her. Pushing each arm to the side, they easily pulled away. Basic self-defense.

At Greta's surprise, Kat sneered. "You're not the only one with supe powers." With that, Kat hiked her leg up and kicked the dhampyre in the stomach. The woman flew back, sliding on the floor.

Immediately, Kat crouched next to him. Her hand cupped his cheek, turning his head toward her. "Thank you."

He wondered what she gave gratitude for. He'd done nothing to help her. He couldn't even keep her safe. Behind her, Greta climbed to her feet, face snarling. Panic roared through him, but he couldn't tell his mate to run, to get away. He was completely helpless.

She winked at him. "I got this." Movement next to his thigh caught his attention. In her hand, she held a broken piece of the chair — a wooden stake.

Greta moved at vamp speed, scaring him. How could a human react fast enough?

Kat swiveled on the balls of her feet, rotating around with the wood shard braced in her straightened arms. As Greta lunged at her, the dhampyre impaled herself around the weapon. His mate and Greta rolled over him, Kat coming up to push the stake all the way through the vamp's body.

Greta screeched, grabbing at the scrap of wood, but quickly fell back, dead. He breathed out, relieved his mate was strong in more ways than one. And his.

* * *

Kat had draped a piece of Hunter's torn clothes over his lap. During her digging, she came across a dart like the kind that held tranquilizers. He had to have been shot with it. She was scared shitless. Hunter didn't seem able to talk or move. Only his eyes worked. Was he dying? If only the dead bitch could talk.

When the vamp dove at her, she felt the piece of wood embed itself in the woman's chest, but when rolling along the concrete, Kat knew the job hadn't been finished. Not until she felt the life leave the bitch's body did she let herself relax.

With Greta's death, her mind control over the men vanished. They surrendered to Brock and the police. The boss had Sway and Cash dragged out and taken to the shifter hospital or wherever they went. He now stood over her and Hunter.

"What happened here?" Brock asked.

Kat shrugged. "I'll give my statement later. We need to find out what Hunter was injected with." She handed the dart to Brock. He sniffed it.

"Never smelled it before." He pocketed the weapon. "I'll have the men cart Hunter to the med lab."

The sweet voice she longed to hear spoke beside her. "Bullshit," Hunter slurred, "I'm not being some pin-cushion rat for your experiments."

Brock smiled. "There's the man we know and love. Well, at least you, Mejia."

Oh God. Her face erupted in flame. She'd never told him how she felt about him.

Brock turned and walked away, saying over his shoulder, "Don't worry, Mejia, you're the only one who didn't have a clue how much he loves you. We all have mates."

Was that what she'd felt? Earlier, when lying on the ground, every muscle ached. Her head wouldn't stop spinning and her ribs poked her lungs with every inhale.

Then suddenly she felt an. . .essence. . .in her heart, asking for her to open. Instinctively, she knew this was Hunter asking her to love him. That he wanted her to be a part of him forever.

She let herself take in his connection and felt a link snap into place. Tingly energy zipped through her body. The aches and pain disappeared. She could breathe deeply again. Looking around, she noted the woman bending over her man's cock was about to be gandar fodder. The quickest, easiest weapon she had was the chair, which worked out very well.

Now with Hunter getting better, she let her anxiety go. His hand lifted to her face and he pulled her toward him for a kiss so hot, she was sure her undies were soaked.

He pulled back, leaving her wanting more. He said, "How about we get out of here?"

Her brow raised. "And how do you suggest we do this?"

His grin was so adorable. "Whatever Greta had cooked up is wearing off." He let out a sigh. "My dragon is back and wanting you to himself for a long time."

"I think I like this dragon. How do I meet him?" she asked.

His grin turned into a smile. "Give me a minute and you'll get the ride of your life."

She laughed wondering what he meant by "ride."

EIGHTEEN

There was no way she could've known that
saying yes to Hunter's simple question
would've landed her on the back of a dragon or
in another country. Sleeping most of the way and
allowing the healing magic of her mate's dragon
to finish restoring her bruised and battered body,
she awoke to a candlelit dinner on the highest
terrace of Hunter's castle.

Shock and awe didn't begin to describe how
she felt, and then there were the nerves. She'd
been sure she would catch the sleeve of her dress
on fire, say the wrong thing, or spill the wine, but
it was a dream come true. She and Hunter had
talked until the sun came up then made love until
it went down. Kat thought back to the hours they
just spent in bed.

"Sweetheart – "

She shook her head and undid his fly and shoved her hand into his jeans. "Mmm, you're really hard."

"Fucking hell!" He groaned, growing harder at the feel of her hand around his cock, teasing him and jerking him in her hold.

She bit her bottom lip and gave him a look full of heat.

He claimed her lips, thrusting his tongue into her mouth and loving the taste of her. He'd never tire of her. Never tire of hearing her little moans when he kissed her or the way she curled her tongue over his, rubbing his and trying to drive him fucking insane.

He removed her clothes with quick movements, growling softly as her skin was uncovered. With her naked, he could feel and touch her silky curves. Her skin felt warm and so soft, he could touch her forever.

She yanked his jeans down and jerked him in her grasp. Sucking one of her nipples into his mouth, he slid a hand between her warm thighs and was greeted with liquid heat dripping from her center.

"Fuck, Kat," he groaned and dipped a finger deep inside her. "You're so goddamned wet."

She moaned, raking her nails over his shoulders and rocking her hips into his hand so he could go deeper inside.

"Fuck me," she breathed. "I dreamt you made me come on my dragon ride. Make it a reality now. I woke aching for you."

He flipped her, draping her over the bed. She shoved her ass back, spread her legs wide and clung to the headboard. He didn't wait. She was slick and more than ready for him.

He drove deeply until he was balls deep inside her. Her pussy fluttered around his length. "God, baby girl. You're so damn hot and the sucking sounds your pussy's making is driving me crazy."

She whimpered and pushed back to each of his forward drives. He gripped her hip and shoved her hair over her shoulder, kissing the back of her neck. Her pussy tightened around his dick, making it almost impossible for him to pull and surge deep.

"Faster," she panted.

He gave in, increasing his speed and drive. The sound of skin slapping, her moans and his grunts filled the bedroom. He bit the back of her neck.

She turned her head and he kissed her ear lobe.

He fucked her hard, his mind full of the idea that she was his and his alone.

She held the bedframe in a white-knuckle grip. "Oh my god, Hunter. Please. I'm so close."

He went deeper. As deep as he could while pulling her ass into each of his thrusts. Then he licked her ear. "I don't have time to give your gorgeous ass the fucking it needs right now, but I'll get you off so hard you'll never doubt who you belong to."

He sucked his thumb into his mouth and pushed

it into her asshole.

She gave a loud groan, her pussy squeezing hard at his dick. He curled his arm around her hip, pressing two fingers over her clit.

"Oh my fucking god!"

He fucked her ass with his thumb and took her pussy with quick drives of his cock. She tensed, her pussy sucking wildly at his shaft.

Then she screamed and came apart in his arms. He continued driving his thumb in and out of her ass at the same time he took her sex. Her pussy walls tightened around his length. He bit down on her shoulder, finally giving in to his own climax. He came hard, his cock pulsing and spilling his seed inside her. His dragon roared, the sound coming out of him in a loud growl. He emptied himself in her and knew there was no way in hell he'd ever let her go. This wasn't just here and now. This was forever.

She couldn't wipe the smile off her face if she tried and she didn't want to.

No longer did the words *arrogant, aloof,* or *unapproachable* describe the wonderful man she would love for the rest of her life. They were replaced with *generous, kind, affectionate, open,* and *honest.*

She would never forget the shy look on his face when she blurted out, "Why were you such an asshole when we first met? The way you glared and avoided me, I thought you hated me."

Looking away, his gorgeous profile intensified in the soft, golden glow of the candles, she'd longed to rub away the lines of tension at the corners of his eyes and the deep frown of his lips. Finally, when he looked back, she'd seen true regret written across his face as he explained.

"Mates were for other people, or so I thought. I'd been a loner most of my life. Damn sure didn't like to share my toys." His chuckle was harsh and full of regret, more of a bark really. "Undercover was a perfect fit for me. I didn't have to look out for anyone but myself. Did what I wanted, when I wanted, answered to the boss, and told the rest of the world to fuck off. That's the way I *thought* I liked it, but dammit it all to hell was I wrong. I was actually dumb enough to think I didn't want or need *you*."

Reaching for his hand, she held on tightly, offering him the support she knew he needed as he struggled to continue. "Then there you were, gorgeous, dynamic, smart as a fuckin' whip and I refused to go down without a fight. Sure, it was useless," he scoffed. "But I fought it anyway."

Lifting her hand and kissing the knuckles, Kat felt his gaze to the very pit of her soul as he whispered, "Thank God, I came to my senses."

Waking to butterfly kisses on her cheeks, down her neck, and across her shoulder for the third morning in a row was nothing short of heavenly. Add to it that she was in an honest-to-God castle in the Scottish Highlands and the only thing better was the man who'd sworn his undying love to her.

Rolling onto her back, she sighed, "You better hurry before my husband gets ba...ooohhhhhhh noooooooooo." She ended up giggling and squealing as Hunter started to tickle her ribs. "Stop stop stop stop stop," she begged with what little breath she had left, gasping when he reluctantly did as she asked.

Running her fingers through his hair and staring into his eyes had become her favorite pastime, and this time was no different. Biting her bottom lip, she went ahead and restarted the conversation they'd been having since they'd arrived at his family home.

"I have more questions."

Flopping onto his back and covering his eyes with his forearm, Hunter groaned, "Already? We haven't even had coffee yet."

Popping up to sitting position, Kat covered herself with the sheet and while running the tip of her finger through the little bit of dark hair covering his nipple, playfully cooed, "I'll make pancakes. With blueberries and honey."

Peeking out from under his arms, Hunter's lips curved into a body-warming grin as he hummed, "And bacon and those scrambled eggs with cheese?"

Leaning down, she placed a chaste kiss on his lips before nodding, "Uh-huh, sure will."

Moving to his side and propping his head on his hand, her gorgeous mate acquiesced, "Okay, hit me, sexy woman."

"When you thought it was Sway, were you really going to kill him?"

"Yes, I was. If he had been the one who hurt you, I would have ended his life without a second thought and never looked back." Shaking his head and letting out a long-suffering sigh, he went on, "But, I should've recognized Greta's scent. Should've known she'd forced him to drink her blood in order to control him. I really want to know what she threatened him with. Had to have been something really important to get him to purchase that nursery, use the computers at FPU to find the girls she wanted, and drive the getaway car all those times. I'm sure those young women are alive because of him." Looking up with half a grin, she knew he was forcing for her benefit, he chuckled, "But the boy's tough. In the end, he shook her control better than that fucking hawk who's at least four times his age."

"Speaking of Cash, you going to be able to forgive him? You guys have known each other for a long time." She pushed on, needing her questions answered. "I mean, he was the one actually kidnapping the girls and telling Greta everything we were doing."

Just as it had been the other times they discussed the hawk shifter, Hunter's eyes flashed a dark, stormy, midnight blue and his pupils elongated just as they had in dragon form. Fortunately, this time, he recovered a little quicker and his voice was less harsh.

"Yes, I forgive him, but I will never forget. Sure, he was under Greta's mind control just like Sway had been, but at least part of him had to be willing. Ya' know what I mean?"

"No, not really. You shifters have a whole load of stuff going on that I've yet to figure out."

"True," he nodded. "But Sway was able to shake the effects of Greta's blood and mental suggestions. It should've taken a sledge hammer and a gun to the head for her to fuck with Cash's brain. Hawks are predators. They rule the roost. He just didn't resist. That's the only explanation."

Scratching at the sexy stubble on his kissable jawline, her mate shrugged. "Maybe it's the lack of family, a mate, no deep ties to anyone or anything, or the combination of everything. I just hope he gets the help he needs." Hunter paused then looked her right in the eye. "What I can't...*won't* forgive is myself. Not yet. If I had killed her when my clan and I were sent in all those years ago to exterminate that entire bloody coven, none of this would've happened. You wouldn't have—"

"Stop," she demanded, swatting his arm. "I won't listen to you take the blame for having a good heart, for sparing a life. Besides, you saved me first. If your *friend* hadn't undone my restraints, things would've ended very differently."

"Yeah, so you keep saying." Love combined with vehemence made his eyes glow a brilliant blue. "But think about it from my side. That bitch came *here* to punish *me*. She had Cash and Sway abduct those girls to make them blood slaves for her coven where I live and work. According to Wyatt, it was her plan to have at least fifty who could feed them and in the long run create a synthetic drug for taking down all shifters."

Moving her hand to his chest and laying it over his heart, she smiled. "I know it's too soon, but some day you'll find a way to forgive yourself. Until then, it's my job to remind you a hundred times a day that you have an amazing heart with an endless capacity to love and accept."

Winking, she added, "Look at us. You never wanted a mate. Did everything you could to scare me off and here we are. You healed me…no, *saved my life* when I didn't even know I was dying."

Wrinkling her nose because she knew it made him smile, she went on, "And, hey, it doesn't even freak you out that I know when people are dead by looking at a picture or touching the same doorknob they touched." Slapping her free hand over her own heart, she chuckled, "And that's a first for me."

Shaking his head and smiling, Hunter sighed. "You're right, I did try to run from having a mate, but it had nothing to do with you, my love. I couldn't run away from you."

Holding up her hands, waving them for him to hush, she imitated his voice the best she could and teased, "I'm just a big, burly, pain in the ass dragon, a loner, and I thought I'd just fuck it all up. I was afraid of hurting you and ending up hating myself."

Squealing when he wrapped his arm around her waist and pulled her onto his chest, Kat shook her index finger and warned, "If you distract me *again*, Mr. Cross, I might not have the strength to cook your breakfast."

Out of the bed, dressing not only himself, but also her, and transporting them into the kitchen before she knew what was happening, Kat held tightly to his arms until the room stopped spinning then snickered, "I'm never gonna get used to how fast you can move."

"Sure you will," he answered over his

shoulder, his head in the huge, stainless steel refrigerator. "You'll get lots of practice."

"Like flying on the back of your dragon?"

"Ah, yep," he winked, placing eggs, bacon, cheese, and milk on the counter. "Cross Dragon Airways is at your disposal, my lady."

Batting her eyes and pretending to fan her face, Kat flirted, "Why Mr. Cross, I do think you're tryin' to spoil me."

Leaning across the counter and kissing her soundly, Hunter pulled back and waggled his eyebrows as he assured, "Every day for the rest of your life."

The heat in his eyes made the bite mark on the side of her neck pulse and her pussy wet with need. Touching the mark, *his mark*, she sighed, "I can't believe we're already married...I mean, mated."

"We are whatever you want us to be." He kissed her again before pulling her onto the counter, sliding her bum toward him until she wrapped her legs around his waist. "Mated, married, lovers, partners, anything you want, I will make it happen."

"Even a big wedding."

"Even a big wedding," he easily agreed. Slamming his lips to hers and kissing her senseless, she moaned at the loss then chuckled when he lifted her off the counter and gave a sexy growl. "Hell with food. You're all I need, Katrina Cross."

NINETEEN

Making it as far as the foyer, Hunter lowered his lips to Kat's. Yes, he wanted her more than he wanted his next breath, but after talking about almost losing her, he needed the reassurance of a slow, passionate kiss.

Tasting first one corner, working his way across her flawless lips, he paid extra attention to her perfect little cupid's bow. The flames that were always burning when Kat was anywhere near roared into a raging fire that only being buried inside her could quench.

Her enticing moans and sweet gasps fed his excitement. His body vibrated with need as her hands slipped under his T-shirt and slid up his ribs. Nails scratching at his chest and digging into his shoulders made rational thought impossible.

Needing to feel every inch of her amazing

body rubbing his, his hands flew across her body. Thank God, he'd dressed her in a nightshirt and not a pair of the abominable sweats she liked so much. Leaning back, he made quick work of her top and gazed at her amazing body.

Dropping to his knees, Hunter's eyes never left hers. Kat was everything *any man* could ever want and thank God, she was all his. Loving that she stood before him topless and confident with a look of unconditional love deep in her hazel eyes was more than he'd ever thought he deserved. His mate knew he found her attractive and dammit it all to hell if that was sthe sexiest thing on earth.

Gently massaging up her well-toned legs in pursuit of ridding her of the one slip of fabric keeping him from worshipping her naked body, Hunter watched as fiery passion filled her eyes. Paying special attention to the tops of her thighs, he teased along the lace of her panties, basking in the heat and succulent aroma pouring from her pussy.

Slipping his hands under the silk at her hips, he slowly slid her panties down her heated skin, following the soft pink silk with soft kisses and the tip of his tongue. Lifting first one foot and then the other to get rid of the only thing stopping him from pleasuring his mate, he kissed the tops of both her feet before beginning his journey back up her body to what enticed him the most.

The higher he climbed, the more Kat involuntarily tried to push her thighs together, but Hunter was having none of it. Gently holding her legs where they were, he kissed the tops of her knees and then moved around to the backs. Trembling as he lavished her tender skin with his lips and tongue, Kat's fingers dove into his hair as she mewled, "Hunter, I love you so very much."

Smiling against her skin, he hummed, "I love you more, Katrina."

Making his way to the tender flesh at the top of her thighs, his gaze was drawn to her lust-soaked eyes. There was nothing like the effect he had on the one and only woman he would ever love. He couldn't help but grin wickedly at the hitches in her breath and the way she moaned his name like her own sacred mantra.

Moisture glazed his fingers when he slipped them between her thighs, the proof of her need flowing freely from her pussy. He was overwhelmed this time, just like every time, with the raw need only she could bring to life within him. Sliding her legs farther apart, he licked the inside of one thigh and then the other, holding tightly as her muscles helplessly tried to close him out.

Blowing small puffs of air against the wet curls that covered her mound as just the tip of his finger teased her outer lips, Kat's nails scratched against his scalp while she pulled his hair and whimpered, "Oh...oh, oh, Hunter, please, please...you're...you're making..."

Evaporating in a wail of pleasure as he pushed first his middle and then his ring finger deep into the warmth of her desire, her body pulled his fingers farther into her depth. Working his fingers in and out, her juices flowed into his hand and down his arm. Every time was like the first time, Kat was so responsive, so beautiful, so amazing that he hadn't stopped smiling since they landed in his homeland.

Watching her head thrash side to side, his free hand on the sweet softness of her stomach was all that kept her standing as her body trembled under his loving touch. Begging and crying out, she panted, "Hunter, please...*please*...I need *you*..."

Loving the sounds of her passion, he needed to wring every last ounce from her. Crooking his fingers in a come-hither motion, he teased and taunted the sensitive bundle of nerves deep inside her at the same time his thumb and forefinger gently squeezed her throbbing clit.

Screams of passion filled the hallway as Hunter held Kat upright and continued working his fingers in and out of her. On and on her climax continued, ebbing and flowing, it was the most miraculous sight he'd ever seen. Waiting as she floated back to earth, her succulent scent filling his every sense, the dragon growled, "And now I shall have mine."

In one fluid motion, he put her legs over his shoulders, placed his hands on her hips, and began to feast. One sip of her nectar was just like the first...every time was like the first time with his Katrina.

Driving his tongue as far into his mate as he could go, Hunter lavished the special bundle of nerves at the top of her channel with the tip of his tongue just as he had his fingers and held on tightly as Kat bore down on his face, rocking back and forth, driving his tongue even deeper.

Their rhythm was frantic. He tasted all of her. The warm sweetness of her arousal flowed down his throat. His dragon roared. Nothing had ever felt so right, so wonderful, so complete in all of his very long life.

The walls of her vagina contracted over and over, faster and faster. Her juices dripped down his chin and onto his chest. He bathed in her scent as he drove his mate to completion, needing to feel her come into his mouth.

Howling as his frenzied tongue flew in and out of her, Kat's wails were unintelligible except for his name. Her hands were once again in his hair. She pulled and tugged until Hunter was sure he was bald and decided it was too perfect a moment to care.

With the force of her orgasm gaining momentum, he could feel her need to completely surrender just out of her grasp. Thrusting his tongue into her then immediately pulling it out, Hunter gently bit down on her swollen nub and held on as she came with such force, it was a miracle they weren't both flat on the floor.

Not letting up, driving his tongue back into her again and again, he licked and sucked and teased, making her come over and over until she was begging, "Please...please...Hunter...mercy...*mercy.*"

But there was none to be had. Hunter needed his mate. He needed to be buried deep within her. Needed to feel her coming around his cock.

Pulling his tongue out of her, he let her limp legs slide down his arms as he got to his feet. Marveling at the sight of his wife gasping for air and her bottom lip red from where she'd bitten it out of the sheer passion only he could give her, Hunter could no longer wait.

Slamming his lips to hers, he used his enhanced reflexes to strip out of his pajama pants. Pulling his lips from hers with a gasp, he lifted her into his arms, and climbed the stairs two at a time.

Working hard to stay on his feet while Kat

placed lazy kisses on his chest, Hunter sucked air through his teeth as she scraped her nails across his raised nipples making his painfully hard cock jump against the soft globes of her ass. A sly grin crossed her lips as the tip of her tongue danced over his chest and she whispered, "Someone's excited."

Crossing the threshold of their bedroom, Hunter stalked across the room, gently laying Kat in the middle of their king-sized, four-post bed. Just about to follow her down and have his way with her, his always surprising mate rolled to her stomach and lifted onto her knees.

Momentarily dumbfounded, he almost came down his leg when she flipped her long mane of curls to the side and looking over her shoulder purred, "Whatcha waitin' for, Agent Cross?"

Needing no more invitation, Hunter went from standing at the side of the bed to on his knees with his hands on Kat's hips. Holding fast with the tip of his cock poised at the warm, wet entrance of her pussy, flames danced along his spine.

Caught in her whiskey-colored gaze, he slowly pushed into her. Inch by glorious inch, closer and closer to being one with the love of his life, Hunter panted as the need to lunge forward battled with the want to savor every single second of entering his mate. However, Kat didn't agree. Taking control, she forced her hips backward, engulfing him in the fiery heat of her depths.

The tip of his erection bumped the mouth of her womb. Her ass slapped against his hips right before all motion stopped. Sighing in unison as her heavenly walls contracted around him, her body pulled him even deeper and held them together before she rolled her hips in the most erotic little figure eight, that made his eyes roll back in his head

The need to move became undeniable. Digging his fingers into Kat's soft flesh, he pounded in and out of her. Rocking on her knees, she met him thrust for thrust. Unbridled passion flowed between them. He couldn't go fast enough, couldn't get enough of her, needed to never leave the haven of his mate.

Leaning his much larger body over hers as they continued to move as one, Hunter palmed both of her ample breasts. Loving the way they swayed in his hands as his body moved in and out of her, he massaged her supple skin with enough force to drive a squeal of pleasure from her lips.

The harder he massaged, the harder her walls contracted around his erection. The erotic massage drove the breath from his lungs. Hunter panted while trying to maintain control with his orgasm threatening to roll over and through him. Needing to climax at the same time as his mate, he tenderly pinched both of Kat's nipples between the thumb and forefinger of each hand then rolled his hips as he thrust in and out with uncontained vigor. The change in position pushed the tip of his cock against the nerves at the top of her channel with every swipe while his hips pushed against her swollen and sensitive nub.

Just when she about to lose control, Hunter could no longer hold out and bit down in the same spot where he'd marked them on their first night together. Screaming his name until she lost her voice, Kat's pleasure had Hunter roaring against her skin and coming with such force, he had to let go of her beautiful breasts and slam his palms onto the bed to keep from collapsing onto her back. On and on their combined ecstasy continued, wringing every drop of pleasure from them both.

Slowing his motions, softly moving with small strokes until both their heart rates returned to normal, Hunter stayed buried deep within his mate. Wrapping one arm around her waist, he reluctantly let his still semi-erect cock slide from the sweetness of her pussy.

Rolling her over in his arms and laying her head on her pillow, he followed her down to the bed and pulled her close. Looking deep into her love-soaked eyes, he whispered, "I love you, Kat Cross."

"I love you more, Hunter Cross."

"Damn, I'm so glad," he sighed. "Cause, lady, I would be lost without you."

Shivering as she ran her finger down the bridge of his nose, Hunter couldn't look away, he never wanted to be anywhere but where she was. Opening his mouth to tell her just that, he ended up barking with laughter when she said, "And I have to ask one more time, are you sure you don't have any other homicidal women from your past lurking about?"

Kissing the tip of her noise she laughed, "Hell no, baby. You're the only homicidal woman for me."

EPILOGUE

"Hello?" Kat answered her cell phone then cursed for not looking at the caller ID.

"How are you? Recovering?" Brock's voice sounded weirdly happy.

"Yes, sir. Thank you for asking."

"I'm glad to hear it. Is your husband there? I tried to call his phone, but it keeps going straight to voicemail."

"Hang on, boss." Pulling the device from her ear, she hit the speaker phone icon while mouthing, *"For you"* toward her hubby who was still in bed. "Okay, sir. You're on speaker phone."

"Hello," Hunter grumbled with a roll of his eyes.

"I needed to give up a heads up, Cross."

"And why might that be?" She watched her mate sit straight up in bed and glare at the phone. "I'm quite literally in another country, across an ocean, what could you need to prepare me for?"

"Did you meet the analyst who connected all the abduction cases? London Connor?"

"No." Hunter's answer was more of a growl. "What's that…"

Knowing her mate was still pissed at the boss, Kat jumped in, "I met her, sir. She's really talented and incredibly intelligent."

"Good to hear. That's what Vega says, too."

The longer than usual pause had Kat looking at Hunter and shrugging before he grumped, "And?"

"And she'll be our newest agent."

"And you thought I needed to know because…" Hunter was frowning and shaking his head. "Let me guess. You're transferring me to Human Resources."

For one of the only times she could recall, Brock actually laughed out loud before asserting, "Hell no! I like my job and refuse to lead more than one asshole like you." Clearing his throat, the boss continued. "I just wanted to let you know that I've spoken with an old friend of yours, Gil Something-Or-Another, the dragon who heads up the Dragon Protection Agency."

"I hate to sound like a broken record," Hunter sighed. "But…and?"

"And he's loaning us your friend Oz to partner with London."

Falling backward and laughing out loud, Hunter guffawed, "Good luck with that, boss. Oz makes me look like Prince Charming."

"Son of a bitch. Why do you dragons have to make life so hard?"

"Everybody's gotta be good at something." Hunter laughed. "Have fun with Oz."

"Go to hell, Cross. Straight to hell."

Hunter hit the end button and tossed the phone aside. "Good morning, my love." Kat could think of a better way to wake up, Brock just interrupted her plans. With that thought in mind she leaned over and nibbled his jaw.

His long, hard cock stood proud, waiting for her touch. With most men, she was unsure about doing this, but with him, it felt natural.

His skin was warm, smooth. She curled a hand around his thick shaft and pumped slowly up his length.

"Ah, fuck, Kat."

She grinned at the desperate way he said her name. Like he was hanging on by a thread. "Tell me what you like."

He lifted his head to meet her gaze. His abs contracted with his movements. "I fucking love everything you do, baby. Every goddamned thing."

She lifted her lips in a smile. "Really?"

"Really."

She lowered to run her tongue in a circle over the head of his cock. A rough growl sounded from him.

"Do you like that?" She did another slow lick and swept her tongue down to his balls, taking each into her mouth and sucking lightly. "Or that?"

He growled. "I love it all, but I'll love your lips wrapped around my dick more."

She snorted a laugh and went back up, taking him into her mouth, letting her spit slide down his shaft and using it to lubricate him as she jerked him in her grip.

"Fuuuck!" he groaned. "Your mouth feels like heaven."

Kat took him deeper, letting him slide in and out of her mouth. He twined his fingers into her hair, grasping her curls. His ass came off the blanket as he thrust his cock into her mouth. Her pussy soaked with every groan and sound he made. She loved that he was enjoying what she did. His pleasure was making her thirsty to have him inside. Beads of moisture gathered at the tip of his dick. She flicked her tongue over it, tasting him. He was salty, earthy. Her body craved more.

She sucked him deeply again, taking him farther. His groans got louder and deeper. She worked him with her hand, jerking him faster, sucking him tighter. His grip on her hair grew painful and the thrusts he made into her mouth suddenly stopped. He gave a loud roar as he came in her mouth, his seed spilling down her throat. She swallowed quickly, taking every drop of him into herself.

She didn't get a chance to think about his taste. He slipped out of her mouth and was sitting up, jerking her hoodie over her head in seconds. Then it was her pants. Soon she was straddling his legs again. He sucked one of her breasts into his mouth, the sensation sending fire shooting to her clit.

"Oh god," she mumbled.

He glided his hands all over her as if unable to get enough of her body. He tweaked her other nipple, pinching and pulling, making her squirm. She leaned forward, pressing her breasts into his face. His lips moved over her skin like a hot brand, taking, tasting, owning.

He leaned back, tugging on her hips. She scooted up until her knees were to either side of his head and her pussy was above his mouth.

"Now this," he rumbled in a sexy low voice that made her nipples tighten, "is what I call breakfast."

He curled his arms over her legs and pulled her down to his mouth. She held on to his hair, unsure of how low she could go without depriving him of air. When his tongue flicked over her folds, she knew she was at the right spot.

He licked at her pussy, rubbing up and down her sex, sucking at her wetness and biting at the inside of her thighs.

She cupped her breasts in her hands, caressing her swollen flesh and pinching at her nipples. Her arousal grew in strength and need coursed through her veins like a drug seeking its target.

He licked and fondled her pussy with his tongue, drawing circles and lapping at her like he loved her taste. She sensed he did. Would bet on him loving her flavor.

Tension curled in the pit of her stomach, winding quickly with every lick he gave her. Every groan and each of her moans only pushed her closer to that moment she knew she'd see stars. Her body shook, making her fall forward to grip the blanket.

He nibbled on her clit and sucked hard, making her fly over the edge. He slipped his tongue into her, fucking her in short, hard thrusts. Pressure exploded inside her and a wave of joy took her by such force, she was left breathless and gasping for air. She choked, her pussy grasping at his driving tongue.

"Oh...oh my god!" she finally got out.

He was at her back in a heartbeat, his cock spreading her pussy folds open and gliding in. He felt massive, filling her so completely, she swore there wasn't a millimeter of space left. Then he reared back and drove forward, sending fire racing through her pussy.

She moaned, her body aflame with need.

"No matter what happens," he ground out, his cock driving in and out of her like a hot branding iron. "You'll always know I said I love you first."

"Hunter," she moaned, pushing back into each of his thrusts.

"You are mine. You'll be mine no matter what happens," he said on a hard thrust. "Always mine."

He dropped over her, caging her under him.

"Always," she breathed.

He took her faster, harder. He curled an arm around her waist and pressed her back into him. Then he slid that same hand between her legs and pressed at her clit. "Suck my dick with your hot pussy. I want to feel you tighten around me."

She curled her nails into fists on the blanket and let herself go. She screamed this time. Loud. Her pussy clasped tightly around his driving cock. His body tensed, making his movements jerky at the same time she rode the pleasure wave. His thrusts slowed until he stopped completely, his cock pulsing inside her grasping sex.

He filled her with his cum, the pleasure intensifying for her. Her body shuddered as mini orgasms rocked her core. Her pussy continued sucking hard at his cock. They fell on the blanket still linked. On their sides, they stayed as they were, enjoying each other. Unwilling to cut the moment short. "This is a life I can get used to Mrs. Cross."

THE END

ABOUT THE AUTHOR

New York Times and USA Today Bestselling
Author

Hi! I'm Milly Taiden. I love to write sexy stories featuring fun, sassy heroines with curves and growly alpha males with fur. My books are a great way to satisfy your craving for paranormal romance with action, humor, suspense and happily ever afters.

I live in Florida with my hubby, our kids, and our fur babies: Speedy, Stormy and Teddy. I have a serious addiction to chocolate and cake.

I love to meet new readers, so come sign up for my newsletter and check out my Facebook page. We always have lots of fun stuff going on there.

SIGN UP FOR MILLY'S NEWSLETTER FOR
LATEST NEWS!

http://eepurl.com/pt9q1

Find out more about Milly Taiden here:

Email: milly@millytaiden.com

Website: http://www.millytaiden.com

Facebook:
http://www.facebook.com/millytaidenpage

Twitter: https://www.twitter.com/millytaiden

If you liked this story, you might also enjoy the following by Milly Taiden:

Sassy Mates / Sassy Ever After Series

Scent of a Mate *Book One*

A Mate's Bite *Book Two*

Unexpectedly Mated *Book Three*

A Sassy Wedding *Short 3.7*

The Mate Challenge *Book Four*

Sassy in Diapers *Short 4.3*

Fighting for Her Mate *Book Five*

A Fang in the Sass *Book 6*

Also, check out the **Sassy Ever After World on Amazon**

Or visit http://mtworldspress.com

Nightflame Dragons

Dragons' Jewel *Book One*

Dragons' Savior *Book Two*

Dragons' Bounty *Book Three (coming soon)*

A.L.F.A Series

Elemental Mating *Book One*

Mating Needs *Book Two*

Dangerous Mating *Book Three*

Fearless Mating *Book Four*

Savage Shifters

Savage Bite *Book One*

Savage Kiss *Book Two*

Savage Hunger *Book Three*

Drachen Mates

Bound in Flames *Book One*

Bound in Darkness *Book Two*

Bound in Eternity *Book Three*

Bound in Ashes *Book Four*

Federal Paranormal Unit

Wolf Protector *Federal Paranormal Unit Book One*

Dangerous Protector *Federal Paranormal Unit Book Two*

Unwanted Protector *Federal Paranormal Unit Book Three*

Deadly Protector *Federal Paranormal Unit Book Four*

Paranormal Dating Agency

Twice the Growl *Book One*

Geek Bearing Gifts *Book Two*

The Purrfect Match *Book Three*

Curves 'Em Right *Book Four*

Tall, Dark and Panther *Book Five*

The Alion King *Book Six*

There's Snow Escape *Book Seven*

Scaling Her Dragon *Book Eight*

In the Roar *Book Nine*

Scrooge Me Hard *Short One*

Bearfoot and Pregnant *Book Ten*

All Kitten Aside *Book Eleven*

Oh My Roared *Book Twelve*

Piece of Tail *Book Thirteen*

Kiss My Asteroid *Book Fourteen*

Scrooge Me Again *Short Two*

Born with a Silver Moon *Book Fifteen*

Sun in the Oven *Book Sixteen*

Between Ice and Frost *Book Seventeen*

Scrooge Me Again *Book Eighteen*

Winter Takes All *Book Nineteen*

You're Lion to Me *Book Twenty*

Also, check out the **Paranormal Dating Agency World on Amazon**

Or visit http://mtworldspress.com

Raging Falls

Miss Taken *Book One*

Miss Matched *Book Two*

Miss Behaved *Book Three*

Miss Behaved *Book Three*

Miss Mated *Book Four*

Miss Conceived *Book Five (Coming Soon)*

FUR-ocious Lust - Bears

Fur-Bidden *Book One*

Fur-Gotten *Book Two*

Fur-Given Book *Three*

FUR-ocious Lust - Tigers

Stripe-Tease *Book Four*

Stripe-Search *Book Five*

Stripe-Club *Book Six*

Night and Day Ink

Bitten by Night *Book One*

Seduced by Days *Book Two*

Mated by Night *Book Three*

Taken by Night *Book Four*

Dragon Baby *Book Five*

Shifters Undercover

Bearly in Control *Book One*

Fur Fox's Sake *Book Two*

Black Meadow Pack

Sharp Change *Black Meadows Pack Book One*

Caged Heat *Black Meadows Pack Book Two*

Other Works

Wolf Fever

Fate's Wish

Wynter's Captive

Sinfully Naughty Vol. 1

Don't Drink and Hex

Hex Gone Wild

Hex and Kisses

Alpha Owned

Match Made in Hell

Alpha Geek

HOWLS Romances

The Wolf's Royal Baby

The Wolf's Bandit

Goldie and the Bears

Her Fairytale Wolf *Co-Written*

The Wolf's Dream Mate *Co-Written*

Her Winter Wolves *Co-Written*

The Alpha's Chase *Co-Written*

Contemporary Works

Mr. Buff

Stranded Temptation

Lucky Chase

Their Second Chance

Club Duo Boxed Set

A Hero's Pride

A Hero Scarred

A Hero for Sale

Wounded Soldiers Set

If you enjoyed the book, please consider leaving a review, even if it's only a line or two; it would make all the difference and would be very much appreciated.

Thank you!

Made in the
USA
Monee, IL

14367605R00095